I, autodidact
M S F Johnston

Published by Ceramicon 2020
Malvern, Worcestershire,
United Kingdom.

Printed and bound by
Aspect Design
89 Newtown Road, Malvern,
Worcs. WR14 IPD
United Kingdom
Tel: 01684 561567
E-mail: allan@aspect-design.net
Website: www.aspect-design.net

A copy of this book has been deposited with
the British Library Board

Cover Design Copyright © 2020 Ceramicon

ISBN 978-1-5272-7125-8

Prologue

Beach volleyball is what Terpsichore chooses for the other eight muses when it's her turn to offer them a distraction. Dance and music are her passions, so captaining her team against Melpomene, the muse of Tragedy, has the double benefit of letting Terpsichore practise her moves, attitudes and fetching poses, whilst encouraging her team to be light on their feet at the same time, musical accompaniment provided by Aeolian harps. She would love to get real and work up a sweat but here, supernatural, she has to do without and content herself with giving her sisters winsome female forms, dressing them in flattering garments, and having a good game.

It's half-way-through a match and they're taking a break. She's making her team rub down with own-brand Mount Parnassus fluffy white towels, the fluffiest and whitest there are, although they don't need to, and having a team talk. Melpomene walks off the pitch with Thalia, the muse of Comedy, in tow and approaches Kleio, muse of History, who's sitting on a low wall, looking down at what's going on below. Kleio never wants to join in. This suits everyone as it's four against four and they've all got used to their positions. Kleio's been having a tough time; Kalliope's epic poetry has been keeping Kleio's more prosaic contributions in the shade for a long time: a golden age of history had once seemed possible but Kleio's library in Alexandria was hit by repressions, conflagrations and finally utterly destroyed, which was a huge setback, letting Kalliope back in the game. The later nineteenth century had offered hope of a new dawn but now it was always history through a prism of banalities, like cheese or glue, or worse – humourless tomes where every second word had a footnote, reference or citation and a lot of the writing was simply appalling. Where had it all gone wrong? Was it all over for ever?

Melpomene: 'Darling, we know you've been having a hard time, it's not really Kalliope's fault that she was so popular for so long.'

Kleio: 'Don't worry about me, she's not doing so well now either.'

Thalia: 'History never ends, you can...,'

Kleio: 'Tell that to Fukuyama and all the rest of the dullards who took him seriously. Now it's all cheese and glue.' (Kleio's anxieties had been made well-known to all.)

Melpomene: 'Yes, yes, we know all about that, but we think we've found something for you. It was Thalia's idea and I've looked into it, and I think she's got something. Go on Thalia.'

Thalia: 'Yes, you've been let down for sure but it's still going on down there, even if they're doing it wrong. You need..., you need...,'

Melpomene, interjecting vigorously, impatiently: 'You need to be transgressive and find a new way. We've got someone. Go on Thalia.'

Thalia: 'Yes, we can do it as a joint-venture, minimise the risk that you'll be disappointed. You, me and Melpomene. We've got someone in mind.'

Kleio, aroused: 'Who's that?'

Terpsichore, calling out from the volleyball pitch: 'Can I be in too?'

(Kleio, Melpomene and Thalia sigh inwardly. Terpsichore has convinced herself that any of the muse's projects can only benefit from being enhanced by her interpretative dance and/or music.)

Thalia and Melpomene together: 'Yes, but not in a main way.'

Terpsichore: 'Thanks guys.' (She's finished her rub down and is limbering up with a quick six-pose set of repetitions.)

Kleio: 'Who's is it then?'

Melpomene: 'There's this he...,'

Kleio: 'I'd prefer a she to a he. There's been too much he-ing and it's time for a change.'

Melpomene: 'We've got this he for now, we could easily get a she but right now we've got a he. He's lived a bit, been tenderised and I think he's ready...,'

Thalia: 'Yes, he's been tenderised, and marinaded in life's bitter-sweet sauces, so now he's ready for the barbecue.'

Kleio: 'Thank you Thalia, you're so lurid. Melpomene, what's the bottom line on this one?'

Melpomene: 'He's gone inwards and keeps thinking backwards.'

Kleio: 'Ok. More.'

Melpomene: 'He's had jobs in different areas but not a proper career in any of them and when he got Covid 19...,'

Kleio: 'Is he robust enough?'

Melpomene: ' Yes. It was some year's ago. Anyway, after he had it, he didn't want to go back to being a teacher...,'

Kleio: 'A teacher?'

Melpomene: 'Yes. Kleio, it would be easier if you would let me get on with it. Anyway, he didn't want to go back, so he mostly spends his time in a day-dreamy fantasy world because he reads too much.'

Kleio: 'History?'

Thalia: 'And plenty of it. And when he's not reading about it, he's looking back on his own life trying to make sense of it, but can't. His parents have become historical and he's starting to think that he's next, like he's waiting for the end.'

Melpomene: 'Thalia! Stick to comedy, you're no good at this. He's not "waiting for the end"; he's at an existential point waiting for the end to start; there's a massive difference.'

Kleio: 'But why he? There's countless hes and shes like that.'

Thalia: 'Yes, but we thought we could all get together and get him to do one of those history things you keep going on about.'

Kleio: 'Yes ok, but why him?'

Melpomene: 'He's literally got nothing better to do. Dramatically speaking, it's perfect. He's waiting for something to happen, but doesn't know it.' (Melpomene is obsessed by structure.)

But Kleio was not convinced. It seemed weak. She was happy enough sitting there, thinking about the old days. She would have to give up her moody posturing, rouse herself from her paralysis of indecisive lethargy and engage. It sounded tiresome but there was temptation nonetheless. If it turned into cheese or glue, or risked degenerating into learned but dense nonsense, then she could walk away. It was low risk and the cost of entry was minimal. She could afford it.

'And we've got boots on the ground,' Thalia was straining for a tipping point.

'He could get the ball rolling,' Malpomene pushed against it, and it tipped.

'Ok, we'll give it a go. It's you, me and Thalia, and Terpsichore wants a bit of the action so throw her a bone will you, and I don't want it too dark Melpomene.'

'I promise.'

'And I'm in charge.'

'Yeah, ok.'

'So where is he?'

'That's him there. Can Melpomene pop the cork with one of her portenteous verses?'

'Don't see why not.'

I, autodidact

Do not think the past another country;

Return, yours cannot be their story when

The living are blind and the dead still see.

1

'You have no history,' she said turning the page 'but the nurse has put in your notes that you seemed defensive and a bit introverted when you had your blood test done.' Dr Barass was bringing the consultation to a close.

But Damian had too much history. There were too many incidents, episodes and chapters, stretching too far back, and he was too often surprised by how much history had been piling up over the years. At a certain but unknown moment in the future, its cardinal points would be set down and held as a record in a database. No copperplate entry in a big bound ledger for him, no yellowing documents in a manila envelope, nor even a resting place as a sheet of paper in a proper filing-cabinet. He would be digitised and all alone, tumbling around the datasphere, for ever.

'What does that mean?' he said glumly.

'Your blood pressure and pulse are both too high and way beyond acceptable tolerances so I think it better if we change the medication you're on for the moment and just look at the incipient hypertension.' Incipient sounded nasty. Hypertension sounded chronic. He'd put off getting it looked at for years and four months' treatment hadn't cleared it up and now they'd widened their interest in him and found other 'issues' after the well-meaning nurse had improvised an 'I'll just check your pulse' gag out of the old needle-in-the-arm routine. He was being scooped up good and proper as befitted his new medical profile and, if they knew all, his actual lifestyle.

'Let's try you on these for a while and see if we can't make a difference,' continued the medic.

'Yes thank you but that other bit, the bit about the nurse's notes?'

'Yes, there are some notes. Yes, the notes say that you were a bit defensive and seemed introverted when you had your blood test.'

'I don't really see why.'

'It's nothing to worry about at the moment. Nobody really knows why. People just get that way, especially at your age. There's an initiative going on and a drop-in team is with us right now. You can see them straightaway if you like. They can take you through it at reception. It's all about early intervention before a long-term condition develops – there's no need to put up with it or have it turn into something more worrying later,' and more expensive, thought Dr Barass, a generalist familiar with the means, modes and medians of medical economics, 'so I hope you can spare us a little of your time today Mr Email, they'll point you in the right direction at reception.'

'Thanks Doctor I'll do that' he said, rising to leave, the appointment over and he, as always, keen to gift a doctor with some extra time in their busy day to do with as they liked. Damian closed the door and patted himself on the back for getting it over with so quickly as per usual but this time he visualised a green dot appearing on a radar screen in a darkened room, an anxious query followed by a command, tactical protocols kicking in, tracking beams being vectored to get a fix on his position. Not bloody likely. It was enough getting the hypertension verdict. No bloody way. Time to clear off.

Engage the purposeful stride! Stride engaged. To the door!

'Dah duh dah dah da dah dahh,' Damian liked to give himself musical accompaniments and this time it was the opening notes of the 633 Squadron theme, then came the main bit: 'da-da-da-da-da-da-da-da duh dah.' At the door, 'da-da-da-da-da-da-da-da dah duh.' A flick of the control column, a dash of rudder and back a step to the big green button. Press the button.

'Bombs gone!' To the door again, through the door and full throttle now, climbing and banking away.

'OK skipper, let's head for home.'

'Wilco,' from the navigator,

'Roger,' from the flight-engineer. Status quo ante had been achieved, or nearly, apart from the heart-rate and blood pressure prescriptions and the defensiveness nonsense. He was out and nearly away.

'Hi!' came a loud call from the other side of the car park. Damian turned to look. He knew him. It was someone he'd worked with from before, from years ago, Asthal-Staines, but his name, his first name, what was it? He needed it right now. Damian had to work hard to remember names and often used a trick to help but what trick had he used? Was it something about how he looked, or was it something else; a rhyme, a pun, a possible school nickname? Yes, the last name was right there in front of him, coming up to him, Asthal-Staines, but his name..., what was his name, his first name. Quickly please, come friendly name now! Please!

'Hi!' Damian shouted back.

'Damo!' He was on his way over. 'Damo! I don't believe it!' He was coming up to him all beaming and friendly gestures. 'That's amazing, what are you doing here?'

Name! Name please now! Asthal-Staines was lit up with vital energy and shared it with Damian in a kind of hug.

'Spirogyra, or "your little operation", as you used to call it, have picked up an NHS contract and I'm here for the implementation phase. We've come a long way. You should have come with us when we left Damo. You really should. Dave's done great at picking up business.'

Yes, there'd been Dave as well. Dave Natch and somebody Asthal-Staines. They'd started 'Spirogyra' together. Dave and…, and…, and…, something to do with pond life? Amoebas?

'We're doing well now, really well. We've got national contracts giving support services to the NHS under the 'Wellbeing-You!' mental health initiative, we did the name as well, and our main man here is sick so I've jumped in.'

Damian scrambled for the man's name: sick…, sick…, Dick! Not Dick. No. Arsey? R.C? R.A.C. Rack? Damian's permutations clicked; there was a match and three green lights lit up in a row.

'Rick! Rick. It's great to see you,' gushed Damian, 'How's it going Rick?'

'What a surprise to see you here, like I said, it's going great. I'm just out for a quick smoke. It's quiet at the moment, we can get a cup of tea, what brings you here? Sorry, inappropriate.' Rick chortled at his own gaff and carried on babbling away whilst wrapping Damian up in his personal force field and charming him back into the building on a wave of charisma; the door snapping to attention and opening to let them inside – Rick's presence alone seemingly being sufficient authority.

Damian was now back in the medical centre, in a too-bright meeting room off the entrance foyer, having a warm and laughy man-chat with good old Rick from Marketing as if his wallet had been beguiled from him by a mind-bending TV magician and he, though fully conscious and aware throughout, had been powerless to stop it. It felt good talking to him though. Those days had seemed to be long gone but here was Rick, absolute proof that they had happened and that he'd really had another life. Rick could be a witness if he needed one. Remembrances dripped through the leaky roof of his recollection.

They hadn't been in the same department but work had thrown them together from time-to-time for week-long trade fairs and conferences where you could easily make a show of working and then let it out in the evening and have some fun, and Rick had always been fun to be with. Memories formed out of thin air like clouds streaming from the tops of mountains.

Those mornings were sometimes difficult and they used to get more and more difficult as the conference or trade fair went on, so you could try and fix it by having a decent lunch with a customer, which would help, and then you'd ease your way through the rest of the day with some light banter until the heavy-duty evenings and nights came round again. It was definitely a test of character. Rick could always make it to the last after-midnight round at the bar. So could Damian. That was the moment of greatest danger: when things speeded up and the next thing you knew it was two, or three in the morning. Or even later sometimes. Spain was the worst for that, no question.

Did that still happen? Did people still do that or had times changed? Once a guy he'd met at a hotel bar had talked about an international fellowship of runners called 'Hash'; a non-secret international society who would go for runs together. You could go on a business trip somewhere in the world and meet up with people who wanted to go for a run and you could join in. That was the point of it. That was what Hash was for. Seemed a bit weird. The guy went away a lot and could nearly always get a run in, with other people. Even Ethiopia was no problem apparently. Hash kept him going. Lucky him.

What was it like now everyone was running? Would he have done a run himself if then was now? When would he have gone – before or after breakfast? Or before dinner? Would they go for a run, then have dinner, and go back to the bar, or go running before breakfast? Before breakfast? No way! Breakfast had been the hardest part of the day and sometimes they'd been pretty grim affairs. Very terse. Very taciturn. Damian liked to have his breakfast before everyone else so interactions at that sensitive time could be kept to a minimum. Things probably had changed. Rick was nattering and Damian was nodding along. He became aware that he had a cup of tea in one hand and half a biscuit in the other, the rest of it being mush in his mouth. He slurped some tea from his cup and washed it down and away. Damian was back in the room.

2

Damian told him a bit about himself and what he'd been
up to since they'd worked together and Rick did the same,
going on in his well-practised patter to explain that as the
post-pandemic inquiries had identified anxiety, or 'wellbeing'
as it was now supposed to be called, 'we try not to use the
"A"-word anymore, it's self-perpetuating,' as an absolute
concern to be classified as a major public health issue which
needed addressing. Lots of cash was flowing into the sector,
previously somewhat of a backwater, but now an absolute
boom town. Multiple action-plans, initiatives and projects
were being launched, often funded by the extremely wealthy,
often fronted by the extremely well-known, and it was going
really, really well. Damian went along with Rick; he'd seen the
increasing coverage on the telly, radio and in the papers, those
kind of uplifting posters were all over this medical centre and
in lots of other places he went to.

    Rick filled in: it was a popular tax offset amongst the rich
because it seemed so right-on without being at all left-wing
and was more agreeable for them to support than more
painful and distressing causes. The Covid-19 recession had hit
national finances hard and the health service was, like everyone
else, short of money, so barriers to bolt-on services from
private providers had come down and, as long as it was free to
the public, you were very welcome to pile on in. It was win-
win. Rick was keen to get his local team up and running and
was here to supervise the start-up but had had to get hands-

on when his colleague had called in sick. Rick explained that he was more of a back-end guy but it was a welcome opportunity to get down and dirty at the front-end for a change. 'Make sure you wash your hands though,' thought Damian, mindful of clinical protocol and not being able to help it.

'Maybe that's what happened to me?' volunteered Damian, using his patented 'I've got nothing to hide' french look: palms up, shoulders hunched, eyebrows raised, a slight pout of the mouth – which he called doing 'le bof'', or 'boffing'.

'What did?'

'That happened to me just now. A nurse told the doctor that I was stand-offish or something. It was in my notes.'

'That's what I'm talking about, in fact that's great, it's embedded in this practice's practice. Which nurse was that?'

'Um…,' he didn't like describing people, especially women, to others, as it seemed somehow rude and he liked to think himself a feminist, 'I don't know. It was a lady, about my age maybe.'

'That's great!' Rick pictured a keen professional: a training work-shop, eager, quick to participate, easy manner with the flip-chart, confident in the team-building group activities – possibly recruitable, and made himself a mental note to find out who it was and bag them. 'That's really great,' but something was troubling Rick. Something was not in the right place. There was something missing in the Spirogyra critical pathway.

'Didn't you see the doctor? Didn't he refer you to us?' Damian started to mumble a rambling answer; a strategy which had never proved effective for him because it gave the other party plenty of time to come back in. Rick had well-honed skills and engaged with the opening he'd been given, sensing an outcome. 'No, no, of course it's absolutely voluntary, it has to be, but there are provable benefits, we have data.'

Damian retreated. There is the 'flight' response and there is the 'fight' response but there is the more socially acceptable third way: that of 'stillness', the stillness of the shrew, the questing vole that plays dead. He'd found the name for it on the internet: 'tonic immobility', also called 'thanatosis'. Thanatosis was a word that dried the mouth too much but tonic immobility bubbled in the mouth like a refreshing drink when you said it, so he stuck with that one and it had served him well over the years. You could use it to stop time and when time started again the danger would have gone. Well not always, but there was a good chance and it had often worked.

'Move on Rick. Move on Rick,' telepathy might make a difference, a nudge in the right direction but Rick, unwittingly playing the cat to Damian's mouse and wittingly not wanting to move on at all, helpfully pulled up the on-line Wellbeing-You! diagnostic tool on his laptop, completed the registration details in a tapping blur and invited Damian to sit in the chair in front of it, purring all the while. Time had moved on to Damian's disadvantage and Rick explained the task he'd set up for him to do.

The survey-style assessment would quantify the client's level of wellbeing and identify any concerns, issues or problems it detected. There actually wasn't much to it. You had to rate your general well-being from 0 to 10 and then answer a couple of vague questions along the lines of:

– 'Was there anything that you found particularly challenging?' and if there was something:

- 'Was there some particular support that you could think of to help you with whatever you thought was challenging?' and at the end,
- 'Was there any further support for your needs you could think of and did you have any additional comments?'

Damian saw through it at once. It was typical of the universal fetish for feedback that was bedevilling the world. The questions were deliberately vague to put you off your guard, to lull you into a false sense of security and he wasn't going to make a machine his new best friend at this time or any time. Rick was politely looking the other way and intent on his smartphone. Damian wrote:

'5', 'No', 'No' – and the last bit? – the last bit was always the hardest. Did he have any additional comments? Another 'No' would be too obviously negative but he wanted to make his mark. What to write? What to write? On impulse, and feeling one-up as he did it, he wrote: 'Apparently I have no history'.

Take that robot! Another clandestine blow from the resistance. No sooner was it submitted than a creeping unpleasantness entered his entrails. Damian liked to be decisive and not shilly-shally about, but had his very decisiveness made him appear ever so slightly, dare he say, defensive? Had he handed them a golden opportunity – opened a little door for them, helpfully, and from the inside? Had he made himself out to be a bit…, a bit…., the unpleasant gut-feeling bottoming out and settling into a steady throb, … a bit peevish?

'Thanks Damo, you'll get an email from us down the

line. What do you think of the gig? We're doing the whole thing from soup to nuts. I'm really proud of it, it's the big breakthrough we've been waiting for. The Wellbeing-You! slogan is courtesy of Dave, all credit it to him, but the exclamation mark and the chip were my idea.'

'Chip?'

'Sorry, hyphen. It's just jargon. Sometimes it just needs a fine touch at the end to push it over the edge – to get from good to great. Classy, yes?'

'Clunky, yes,' snided Damian to himself. Rick's all-round enthusiasm was a pick-me-up for a while but it always, he remembered, ended up wearing thin. Maybe he'd found it easier to put up with that kind of stuff before. Maybe he had been more easygoing then, but shouldn't Rick have turned out a bit better dressed if he was going to be front-facing and deal with the public? Rick still had the same look now as he'd had years ago; his shirt always looked like the evil doppelganger of another one left behind, bound and gagged, in a cupboard, no tie and a light grey jacket and trouser combination like an old-school wedding suit, even down to the grey loafers. Rick didn't seem to have changed much. Where could you get those suits now? He looked like he lived in a car and liked it. The two former colleagues began the standard leaving routine.

'Rick, it's been great to catch up – you haven't changed. We should get together some time.'

'You neither Damo, it's been great.' Rick was just about to say 'Don't be a stranger,' when there was an alarming bleep followed by a series of chiming pings from the laptop to which Rick was immediately attentive.

3

'This is about you!' Damian was phlegmatic – it had been about him all day long, it seemed, so why would it end now? 'It's a priority intervention advisory notice, I think. I don't normally handle this myself, well I've never actually…, because I don't normally…, but…, yes …, it's about you.'

'Me?'

'Yeah…, I don't think they expect the client to be around when it…, I thought they sort of bagged them up at the end of every session and then zapped them down to base camp for processing. I should know after all…, I was going to find out…, but as you're here…, not sure if it isn't probably illegal.' A pause. Rick was open to particular temptations which it was in his nature to give in to and this was one such.

'Question: do we give a proverbial flying whatever? You're here. I'm here. It's here. Let's do it now, yeah? Turtles all the way down?'

'All the way down!'

'Yeah?'

'Yeah' – an innocent trigger-word from Rick had punched a hole in space-time and worm-holed both men to multiple heres and nows in their pasts where immediate decisions had to be made to seize that particular and special moment – often a drink too far at a bar – 'yeah' being both detonator and explosive charge.

'Yeah, let's do it!' Damian wanted to get it over with in one dramatic moment. Better to do it now with Rick than being pestered from here to eternity by God knew who.

'Oh wow! Wow! Look at that! You've been coded orange, sorry, say again, amber.'

'What's that mean?' said Damian, anxious and self-conscious.

'Amber is good. It's very good. You are a priority but not the top-priority, which would be red, I think. You can access a shed-load of resources and support materials.'

'Is it all internet stuff because if it is, I'm not really…,'

'For sure, but most of it is interactive. It's been proved to be very effective. Do you want to go down the red hole? Take the rabbit pill?'

A cloying and invisible miasmic vapour was rising slowly all around, infecting Damian's flesh with despondency: his forehead had become waxy, his eyes were getting sticky, his vision was hazing, his mind was stiffening and he began to hold his breath. So much for tonic immobility, he'd nearly made it. Toxic immobility more like. Red hole way out. Only way out.

'Yeah go on then Rick,' came as a dry croaking gasp which to Rick sounded just like enthusiasm made flesh.

'I can open it and show you the attachment. No, you open it, then it's all tickety boo. No, I'll do it as it's not to you, but about you. I personally think it would be great to include clients in the process at this stage. I might try and engineer it into an upgrade. This is great Damo, have a look.'

Damian scanned through his report down to the bottom line. He was a fast reader and hoped to get through it on his own before Rick butted in but Rick was quick as well and couldn't resist it.

'What's the takeaway?' asked Rick, moving closer to share a view of the screen.

'I put a 5 on the ranking index which was about how you thought you were, wellbeing and all that, and that 5 is ranked 3 on this other index.'

'Ooh err missus!' Rick dropped another catch phrase from back in the day.

'And I used the word "apparently" which means something…,' Damian fought against repeating 'apparently' with all his might and was successful, '…as it's there with another code next to it as well.'

'It's all algorithms Damo, I'll check the codes, see what they mean.' Rick did something on his smartphone. 'Got it – "Peevish" is the descriptor they use here for "apparently". "Apparently" comes up as "peevish" when you map it to the taxonomy in the guide,' – Rick avoided the obvious for an instant, then embraced it: 'apparently.'

Damian rolled his eyes, partially inflated his cheeks and then puffed them out, making a sound very much in keeping with his feelings which a natural empath would have had no difficulty recognising but Rick just carried on, not being one.

'The 3 is no surprise because a client 5 actually indicates that they're in a state of denial and that's not good – the middle path is not necessarily the mindful path, more the path of self-deception and the opposite of clarity.' Rick had a faraway look and was trying to parrot a rote-learnt phrase he was supposed to know from an inspirational training session he'd attended, whilst visioning it at the same time.

'Obscurity?' offered Damian.

'Obscurity?' Rick, distracted by his visioning, hadn't got what Damian was on about.

'Obscurity Rick…, the opposite of clarity, …obscurity?'

Didn't this kind of wordplay used to come easily to Rick. Lexical dexterity had been his middle name. Damian was also disappointed in the feedback they'd given on him and was beginning to be resentful.

'Yeah, yeah, obscurity.' Rick had been enjoying meeting with Damian but now he'd realised almost too late that he'd underestimated the workload he was supposed to get through that day and that having a chat with Damian was not bringing him any efficiency gains.

'Sorry Damo we're running out of time here, I've got stacks on. Let's get you on the right pathway. What do you think you need to do to make a difference?' Rick was regretting getting involved. Things always started to go wonky when he winged it. 'Yeah I know, it's a problem. You've got no idea what you need and that's a predictable reaction. It actually has already been predicted. Ok, what do you like doing?'

'Doing?'

'Yeah, what kind of things do you like doing in your spare time? There's a list for you to look at, see? Acting, cooking, crafting, bee-keeping, drinking, just kidding, designing – there's loads. Have a look yourself.' Damian needed to escape; he needed to pull the emergency handle, do a zero-zero ejection and bang the hell out. A heading on the screen caught his eye.

'History? What's that there?' Damian had spotted a quick and easy solution. 'History? Can I do that one? I'll do that one.'

'History? History it is then.' Rick clicked the portal button on the screen. 'There's masses of choice; is there anything you see you like the look of?'

'Ummmm…,'

'Tell you what, I've got "Administrator" status, let's go straight to the good stuff round the back.' Rick clicked open a digital sub-folder and scrolled through lines of options, a bit too quickly for Damian to keep up with.

'What's that one? Back! Back! There. "Online inter-course – a symposium", What's that one?'

'I'll find the guide; it's a separate folder, usually at the bottom, there it is.' Rick's mind was wandering, he wanted a get out as well. Damian scrutinised a list of historians, a thumbnail photo to the left and their biographical details to the right. 'You choose one of them to work with. This is a new one so you can be an early-adopter.'

There were many well-known names: Lorna Dune, Kelvin McGrayth, Louis Landscape and so on, top-notch history people with well-crafted reputations and strong media presences, although he hadn't heard of a lot of them. Which one could he do it with, whatever 'it' turned out to be? He wouldn't have wanted to spend a week in a lifeboat with Nick Pinchman, too intolerant and argumentative, nor her, nor him. Who he? Who her? No…, no…, no…. Back to the top of the list. Landscape had been a hero, wrote well but had got flouncy when the Brexit debate was in its final phase, a black mark surely. Kelvin McGrayth? The spirit of the age came and lay with Kelvin at night and their intimate pillow-talk, which he shamelessly and continuously betrayed, had brought him much fame and reward. Intimidating. Definitely too much.

But Lorna. Lorna Dune. Surely if it had to be somebody then it had to be her. There she was, still around, still in denim jacket and cheesecloth, with the same hair, lit warmly from behind by blond-loving sunshine, same kindly blue eyes, same everything. He still remembered her first TV series from over thirty years ago. She would always find the middle way, wouldn't she? Perhaps her middle name was Synthesis? Or Cynthia. It wasn't all about her with her, it would be about you as well. You'd be able to talk to her. It could be nice. And she knew what it was to have to wear a surname that didn't conform to expected norms, as he did, so they'd have that in common.

'What about Lorna Dune?' Damian tried to appear nonchalant but needed this badly. Maybe it was too late? Maybe she was full up?

'No problem – I'll set it up for you and send you the link, are you ok with Wazz?' There was a loud 'whummfff' as his parachute filled out. He was going to make it.

'I used Wazz a lot when we were working from home, we had to do online lessons when the schools were shut in the lockdown.' He imagined pulling a face whilst engaging with the talking heads shuffling along the top of the screen, with a big one in the middle. Well, he could get through it. Lorna was a safe and sure bet. It could, maybe would, be quite pleasant. There was a kind of karma about his choice. He'd read one or two of her books and seen a couple of her documentaries on television now and again but she wasn't on as often as some other showboats were and now there was the chance of a symposium inter-course with her. Would it be like being reunited in some way, after all these years.

Rick thought of asking Damian why he wasn't at school but thought better of it as he needed to wind things down quickly so he did the on-screen necessaries to get Damian on the course and briefed Damian on what to expect and when to expect it. Damian said he was looking forward to it and thanked Rick again, hoping they would keep in touch. The Wellbeing-You! program might actually have come up with a half-interesting pleasurable internet nonsense which could maybe, in fact, be properly enjoyed. Damian was up for it. Tonic immobility had done it again and he congratulated himself for having broken cover and charged down the only plumb in the pie at the last, critical, moment. Rick was seeing Damian out and they said goodbye to each other in the sincere and friendly way which can appear superficial to the cynical.

'Damian it's been great, keep in touch. Follow us on Twitter and Facebook'.

'Will do Rick.' Damian said. 'Fat chance,' he thought, 'I get my kicks in the real world, sunshine, not your fault Rick.' Damian liked him, they'd shared good times, and some bad ones, but his life had moved on. He wouldn't see him again. Finally there came the inevitable parting patter.

'Damo, remember! The sky's your oyster!'

'And yours!'

'And up yours!'

'And up yours too!'

'Cheers!'

'Cheers!'

4

Epsilon Precinct was a blandly-named collection of five 4-storied red-brick residences interleaved with car parks and connected by tarmac walkways, which could have doubled as an out-of-town business park for dynamic solicitors, charities or companies with random three-letter names, like 'BZJ' or quirky ones like 'Juz Sayin'.

Damian didn't mind living there; if he was a bit down, it looked like a sheltered-housing complex or, if he was a bit up, modern accommodation blocks on an RAF base, but he had no complaints. His childhood dream had been to live on the interest of his capital, like a Bertie Wooster, but he'd never had any and reality had grabbed him by the lapels, shoved him against a wall and given him a good talking to. The plot twists in his own story had been unexpected, bewildering, but here he was, taking time out from teaching thanks to a modest and unwelcome legacy – it wasn't quite the dilettante lifestyle he'd dreamt of but, at least he could do his own thing, for a while. Had he deserved it? He must have done. Your character is your fate, they said.

Here was where he was. Beached. It was a bit austere but not crummy, not bed-sit land, although it was mostly bed-sits, he supposed. He quite liked it because it was perfect for in-between people like him, people who had had to take the consequences: one ground-floor room, a bed-settee, a bookshelf-thing dividing off the kitchen area from the rest. Nobody passed the window, set just a little too high to see out of easily. Other people must have been living there but he saw very few of them. It was a nice handy location, almost in the countryside, and he thought it cosy.

Damian had picked up a hot half-chicken, a baguette, mayonnaise and beer on his way back home for his regular Friday-night feast. He liked to sit on the sofa-bed, use a wooden chair as a dining table, and watch television, especially on Friday nights as there was a golden three-hour session of two comedy sit-coms, a comedy panel show with a funny comedy cartoon to start things off. It was worth looking forward to, never disappointed and everything was in place, ready to go. He'd spent the last week brushing up his history ready for tomorrow's on-line inter-course and decided to go googling as his date with TV pleasure neared.

'Doomak' had been a regular search-term for a long time but he'd never had any luck. He'd found it once – at the start – adopted it, and used it, but he'd never been able to find the word itself again. As if it had never existed. As if he had made the word up himself, or imagined it. It was an important word and not one to mislay like that so he would go looking for it occasionally. How was it spelt? Had he got it wrong? Had it been 'dumak', 'dhumak', 'dummak' or maybe some other version? Damian tried everything but the result was always the same and had been for a decade. He could never find it.

Today he made a change. 'Dumak' and its lookalikes hadn't worked so he'd try and link it to something else…, but to what? Link it to Buddhism? Doomak was a bit mystical so try that. No. But that almost looked like a hit! Tweak it. There it is! Hallelujah! Ha-lay-bloody-loo-yah, that's amazing! That's absolutely blinking flipping ruddy effing jeffing amazing. There it was. It hadn't been 'doomak' at all, ever. It was 'dukha', or it could also be called, it said, 'dukkha', with an extra 'k'.

It even had an entire Wikipedia page. 'Dukha' was a word to describe things that were in the way of you getting to some kind of a state of grace such as searching for something you've only just put down, wrangling with computer problems, thinking about something that needed doing and putting it off, losing your glasses. There were all kinds of dukkha but he insisted on still calling it 'doomak' because he'd got used to it, and thought it sounded better.

Doomak was a cut above the quotidian. Maybe it had shades and nuances, like a spectrum, and could include everything: full-on doomak at one end to a tad doomaky at the other. Damian reserved doomak for noticeable intrusions which loomed over the general herd of 'doings' and so tried to save it for these special, but nevertheless frequent, occasions. Doomak were all those things that used you up, stopped you, prevented you, blocked you from pushing through the bushes and brambles to find that sunny clearing called…? What was it called? Leisure? Was that the best word we had for it: leisure? Was it maybe nirvana? Leisure was nice but it could mean lots of different things and it was surely never nirvana.

What was the epitome of leisure? He didn't mean ordinary leisure squeezed into the business of the day somewhere but timeless moments of free idleness; a hot day, the shade of a tree near a brook, where the only sensible thing a reasonable person could do was to loaf around until lengthening shadows reminded them that time had passed and they'd be moved to leave, to walk along a lane aglow with the lowering sunshine, tiny flying creatures spangling light like ethereal atoms, the air thickened with vegetable musk. Shifted along the lane, unhurried. Shifted along to a pub so they could carry on living the evening on the outside tables, until it was dark and the merry bunting lights came on.

Getting the name wrong and losing it for all that time had definitely, been a perfect case-study exemplification of doomak at work in the world in a big way and he would learn from it. Damian and doomak had been reunited again but surely for doomak to exist there must be an anti-doomak somewhere, it's foe and enemy, yang to its yin?

'Thank you again Wikipedia,' the work of a moment, 'the opposite is…,' check the spelling again, 'the opposite is "sukha". The opposite of "dukha" is "sukha". This is coming together. I like it! I… like… it!'

And the telly was good and the chicken was good and the beer was good and the flowers of sukkah flourished and he slept the sleep of those who had found the opposite of doomak. He'd deserved to find it after all that time. It was about time. It was a pity he hadn't found it years ago. It might have made a difference. Maybe things wouldn't have unravelled so much. But it was still sweet, sweet like sukah. But he called it 'soomak', and always would do.

5

Morning, the best part of the day. Early o' clock and if you were lucky – that the coffee was right and the cigarette was right, no hint of a hangover – then you could almost hold that moment in your hands: the warming sunshine, the perfect coffee, the best cigarette – knowing that you could do it again and again, if everything went right, if the variables could be held within acceptable tolerances. It was always worth aiming for. It wasn't always perfect bliss but it could be. It had that potential. You had to want it. You had to make it happen. There was always something there even when it was a bit off, and now he knew what it was. It was soomak.

The right place to capture it was at a particular gate in the nearby field which Damian used to lean on when he was taking it all in, drinking a cup of carefully-made coffee from a flask, before going back to start the doings of the day and he was there now, thinking about the Wazz symposium call with Lorna, which was at nine, so there was plenty of time. Another cigarette perhaps?

Sooooooooomaaaaaak. Soooooooooo...maaaaaaaaaaaak.

Half an hour to go. Get the link from the email. The screen was always full of adverts that slithered out everywhere, even onto his email page. Why? The screen was cluttered with them. Could you get rid of that nonsense? Why would they do that? He had bought some stuff once and the relentless digital world wanted to waste his time and tempt him into buying it again. There was probably a way to get rid of it but he would have to find it and so incur a doomak penalty in the process which was not to be borne. Maybe one day it just wouldn't be there anymore. He hoped that's what would happen.

Damian checked the video. It still worked. The little plug-in camera had come with Chinese instructions at the start of the corona-virus lockdown and by some miracle had functioned properly, after some doomaking, and still did. Well done little fella. There were reams of emails to delete, many begging for feedback. Idiot emails about nothing, just to give him doomak. Get-em-gone! This is where the wrong one gets deleted, so slow down a bit. Ten minutes to go. All ok. The wee wheel-thing was turning over and over. He was ready. He was nearly 'on'. Five minutes. Cigarette? Yes. Roll one quickly. Two minutes. Sound 'Go!' Vision 'Go!' We are 'Go!'

The screen filled with Lorna who was looking for something on her desk and fidgeting about. Other people appeared in small boxes at the top. Where was his picture? Had he properly connected? Ok, that must be the video button, turn it on. His picture popped up. He was back in the game.

'I can see you but I can't hear you.'

'I can hear you but I can't see you.'

There were about 20 people's heads in little boxes along the top of the screen, labelled with their names. The technical complaints continued and Damian admired his own image, taken at an upward and slanted angle, lending it an arty socialist-realism look, which he liked, rather than the others' full-frontal headshots, which he didn't. He'd changed the tune of 'Why are we waiting?' from 'Oh come all ye faithful' to 'Who let the dogs out?' and he hummed it to himself as he often did in similar situations, especially in his car. The new tune fitted uncomfortably with the words. It was not perfect, but the result was more insistent and more suitable to the fast-moving new century:

'Why? Why? – Why? Why?'

Lorna was used to the dishevelled early stage of a tele-conference with amateurs and she used her expertise to clearly and calmly shepherd her flock with practised grace.

'Hello everybody, I'm Lorna Dune.'

Tony cut her off straightaway and his face replaced hers at the centre of the screen. He was from Reconnoyter in Northern Ireland but Damian detected a North-American accent. 'Always ask if they're Canadian if they have a North American accent, same with Kiwi for Australian, surprises them or wins them,' smugged Damian to himself.

Tony had a Canadian accent and was her greatest fan and had been one of her students in Iowa and…, Lorna interrupted him and, using her skills graciously once more, proposed some formalities which would leave casual pop-ins to the end, or better, nowhere, she hoped, she being the moderator and keen to hear everyone's input.

'Thanks Tony, why don't we all introduce ourselves? I'll go first. Hi again everyone, I'm Lorna and thanks for choosing me for your inter-course,' and she went on to talk about her career: her academic posts, what 'History' meant to her and how she loved her student relationships, the excavations, the dig parties in the evenings, the mad and passionate debates, (a much younger Damian put himself in the middle of a summery evening dig party in a parallel universe, were there also love affairs?) how she was, it seemed, back in fashion, but hadn't changed, although now with a family, and how lucky she had been. Damian could see she still had her vital sparkle. She hadn't really changed at all.

That vitality of hers. Could you call it 'boyish' and add it to 'charm'? Boyish charm. Shouldn't it be 'girlish' for her? Girlish charm? It didn't work in the same way and might even be wrong. Youthful charm? No. The 'charm' of youth was not always that obvious, nor even that of boys, come to think of it. 'Boyish' was still the best fit to describe what it was about her he liked. Girlish charm was not the same, although that could be nice too. Would she mind being boyish? Would she be flattered or upset? He didn't want to cause offence. 'Don't say it,' was the advice he gave himself. Then he pleaded with himself not to say it, under any circumstances whatsoever.

'So that's me, let's hear from you. Could you tell us a little bit about you, and what brings you here? Damian dreaded this part, which he'd used himself many times to pad out the content of training sessions, and stepped straight in.

'Hi, my name's Damian and...,'

'Sorry Damian, can we go from left to right across the screen and then we'll know who's next.' Lorna read the name under the picture on the far left. 'Hi Leyla, tell us about you.'

'It's Lee.'

'Hi Lee' said Lorna, fazed.

'It's Lee-lah,' Leyla exaggerated the syllables and pronounced her name as it was said.

'Sorry Leyla, tell us about you'. Damian was miffed and cursed the double ambiguity; how you said Leyla's name obviously wasn't clear from its spelling and Lorna's 'let's hear from you,' had been ambiguous as well. He'd jumped on the multiple 'you's thinking she was talking about him. 'You-all', 'yall' or even 'youse' were useful precautions against such misunderstandings and should be adopted in the English-speaking world to avoid confusion. He listened and watched as people he didn't know said who they were and how they had come to History.

6

'Damian Hi! What do you do – what do you say?' Lorna liked
using her skills to maintain interest during these sessions so
she would try and vary the words she used to invite attendee
contributions, which wasn't easy, but it kept her on her toes,
and concentrating. Damian got the reference to wisecracking
1940's film-noir dialogue. He got it good, but managed to
suppress the 'Save us the boyish charm doll-face,' retort that
was ready on the tip of his tongue. He'd once used 'Back off
lady!' as a joke to an accountant during a stock-take but her
'I have taken massive offence' body-language was immediately
obvious. If he'd been in costume and dressed like a hard-
nosed, no-nonsense 'I live off whisky and burgers in diners,'
private eye clothes, then all would have been well, and funny,
but context is all, he'd learnt. He used to wonder how long
her resentment had lasted.

'Hi, I'm Damian and I'm a historian,' was what he wanted to
say. He was amongst his peers. They were his support group.
He was coming out to them. They would applaud his courage.

'Hi I'm Damian, I'm a teacher and I've always been
interested in history,' is what he said.

'What are you specially interested in, Damian?' He hadn't
really anticipated how he would answer when this inevitable
question came, despite his preparation, preferring to wing it
off the cuff.

'I've got quite wide interests so it's hard to say really. I liked
what you did on the Anglo-Saxons,' he hoped she wouldn't

write him off as a sycophant, 'but now I've been looking at the Whig ascendancy, Henry VIII and Stalingrad. I've just started with Henry VIII and have more or less finished Stalingrad. Stalingrad went well.'

'Looks like you're across a lot of big themes, what are you getting from Henry VIII?'

'Um…, euh…, there's a sort of…. um…, well…, I'm interested in his power, you know…, where did it come from, euh…, his dad was just the last man standing after the…, the euh…, the euh….'

'Wars of the roses?' interjected Lorna, mindful of the need to keep all her audience with her and who liked to sometimes lightly point up weaker contributions with helpful and timely suggestions, as and when required, but careful all the same to let them have their say without interrupting too much.

'Yes.'

'Well there is a lot to look at there, that could be something worth looking at. Thanks Damian.'

'And next up, it's Gary.' Gary was from Sunderland and shouldn't really have been there as his wife had made him do it.

'Why don't you do the decent thing and spare us all then? Get off the line Gary! Go home to your wife. Try other ways of making her happy, why don't you?' – uncharitable thoughts extemporised themselves unbidden. There was that dialect again. Damian had lived in the North-East of England for a while. Surely the way they spoke up there was an authentic relic of the earliest Northumbrian speech patterns. Damian respected accents and dialects. They were like coelacanths flapping around on deck, history alive in the present.

They'd called each other 'dosser' at school to show their

indifference to study and something easy was a 'doss'; there was a French verb "adosser" meaning to lean back – there was also 'creasy' from junior school, where you crossed your fingers behind your back if you wanted time-out from a playground game, which could have come from the French 'croisé', meaning 'crossed'. How had these words and accents got here? Damian was speculating as the remaining participants went through their shtick. Finally it was over and nearly 25 minutes of twaddle had been shared, according to the little clock at the bottom of the screen.

'Our time's nearly up. You've all got great ideas and I'm really looking forward to hearing what you've got to say.' Damian came out of his linguistic and etymological reverie. 'So now here comes the challenge. You've got to find an area of historical enquiry that you feel passionate about, that's the important bit, and prepare an Extended Project Qualification, or EPQ. which we will assess and, if accepted, will earn you a certificate. You'll get a pack of advice and tips on how to go about it from us and there's a Youtube channel to support you. We've got some time for some questions but not many, sadly.'

Eager and animated puppies jumped out of their basket and made for their beloved, yapping joyfully: 'Will you be our supervisor?', 'Was the EPQ accredited?' and 'Could it go towards a masters' degree?' The participants gave Lorna a great send-off with profuse thanks and praise. Lorna was winding things down; people were starting to wave. Damian gave a wave.

'One more thing, remember! Only connect! Excel and go for gold! Thanks everyone, byeee,' and she waved off.

What the hell was that? 'Go for gold!' Asinine, vacuous

claptrap. He hadn't heard 'Go for gold!' in decades, since the first time he'd tried to get a job and went to a big-city employment agency for a meeting. He hadn't understood anything that had been said to him and the man had shaken his hand and said 'Go for gold!' as he was seeing him out and Damian had never forgotten how he'd felt on the pavement outside, having to go for gold from then on. He'd felt the glib emptiness of it then, when the expression must have already been past it, as nobody had used it to him since. Damian felt it hotly, like a slap on the face, and it stung badly.

Ping! The digital info-pack arrived almost as soon as the screen went black with the usual 'Thanks for blah blah...,' 'and 'Could you please give us feedback blah blah blah.'

'Feedback? I'll give you ruddy scummy feedback,' and he did.

Experience? Nought to ten with ten being the highest? That would be zero.

Comments? Easy: vacuous asinine claptrap.

"Is there any way we can...?" This was going too far. He was not going to be bothered to even deign to begin to even consider putting anything here, and left it blank, submitting his feedback with self-righteous panache. It hadn't gone as he had hoped, perhaps there'd been a bit of an overreaction on his part but she'd set him off and anyway, life was too short. It always turned out to be the same old crappy doomaky digital crappiness in the end. Damian was habituated to long-suffering philosophical disappointment and wanted to move on.

There was still the rest of the day to kill. He would lay in some wine and some grub, which he called 'tweet'. No, better. He would get on his Vespa and scooterise the hell around, pick up some tweet and wine somewhere and maybe buy a book, then come back and watch a film: 'Starship Troopers' again? 'Glengarry Glen Ross' again? 'Groundhog Day' again? They never let you down.

Damian had himself a grand day scootering all over the place but the doomak had been piling up unobserved and suddenly erupted like volcanic undersea pillows of doomak-lava, welling up from the depths, cracking open crimson and then being themselves engulfed by others, in a continuous cycle of birth, decay and death.

He'd lost control of the Vespa on a gravelly bend and earned himself a dent, a paint scuff and some soreness in his shoulder. Later on an unfixable breakdown was made more triumphantly doomaky by Damian having left his phone behind, which made everything much more difficult, and it had taken hours to sort out. Eventually, his roadside assistance company had dropped him and the scooter back at Epsilon Precinct.

His hands were washed and scrubbed although still a bit oily, but that would have to do. Wine please, now! Damn! Cork's crumbled. Gently. Gently. Push it in and fish the cork crumbs out later. That'll do. Tweet, get the tweet happening! Forget the films, try T.V. Same old comedians chatting to each other about things that annoyed them. He'd been through too much that day to put up with it. A bit of whisky then?

'Yes please, make mine a double.' And then what? A documentary on the making of 'Apocalyspe Now?' That'll do. That'll have to do.

'You are kidding me. You have got to be kidding me,' there couldn't be a power cut now. 'Bloody typical!' Should he adopt the 'Guernica' pose and do a gurning Picasso face or pull the 'Platoon' posture? Neither. It wouldn't be dramatic enough alone in the dark. Well maybe just a bit. A bit of Guernica. The power came back on. He was being tested. Bedtime. One more first. So what if he was found wanting. Ok, another one. Ok..., then bed. Definitely after this one.

7

Dawn had come to play but been told that Damian was a bit under the weather and wouldn't be coming out that day, maybe tomorrow. Yesterday had had its ups and downs. There had been challenges but he was now reunited with doomak and had picked up soomak along the way as a bonus, so it was all good, if you didn't count the scooter fiasco, and the on-line intercourse let-down. Yes, he should have been up earlier but he was up now and got stuck into the daily doings, even adding a bit of extra tidying up to show who was the boss.

Doings done, there was now a choice to be made: stay in or go out. One, or the other with no wimpy and indecisive middle-way. It wasn't about synthesis; it was about action or inaction. Actually, he corrected himself, that wasn't quite right as both options were effectively actions. It was more like a choice of locations: location A or location B, and they were separated from each other by the front door. Damian pictured the existential anti-hero turning the door handle. He did likewise, and with the other turned the knob of the lock, paused then pulled. The chain was on, so he closed the door, undid the chain, turned the knob of the lock one more time and pulled on the door again. The door opened and he stood on its threshold. On the very threshold is where I stand, he mentalised carefully. He was there. It was now. He was mindful of both.

Damian's mailbox was in a little shelter on the wall outside, just beside his front door and he went back inside for its key, being careful to put the door on the latch as he'd accidently locked himself out before. He came back out with the key and used it to open his mailbox and checked the contents. There was an A4 manila envelope which he took back inside, closing the door, releasing the lock and putting the chain back on.

'That is a quality envelope,' he thought to himself, 'where could you get quality like that these days?' Envelopes weren't what they were. They had become cheap and flimsy things that tore easily. The opposite of what they should be. American stationery was sometimes better, but old-fashioned and a particular orangey-yellow colour, those A4 pads you saw them using on television were bright yellow. Some time ago he'd got a real-life American mail-bag sent to him. A box of books had split on its way from the States and somebody in the US Postal Service had been thoughtful and put it in a sack to keep it all together and sent it on to him. Had it been sewn by jail-birds? Had it been made out of 'burlap', whatever that was? It sounded right. 'Burlap'. Was this envelope American? Clearly it was of superior quality which guaranteed it a place in his stuff where it would develop a rich patina over time to be found one day amongst his effects.

'Mr D Email' was written on it in royal-blue ink but there was nothing else and looked like it had been hand-delivered. Damian would have written 'By hand' on it, if he was dropping it off and not mailing it because just putting a name on was a bit..., what? Terse? Yes. The envelope he liked, but he felt hostility towards it and was aware of his ambivalent feelings. Nothing for it, the middle way it would be then, so he opened it.

A Mr H-D Dolmetscher had written to him from the local

history association, based in the R.A.F.A building, East Street and was asking Damian if he would be so kind as to consider giving of his valuable time to come and meet with himself, Mr Dolmetscher. Lorna, it went on, had asked him to try and make amends as Mr Email had clearly felt let down and disappointed by the inter-course session. Perhaps there had been a misunderstanding and, although Lorna regretted that she couldn't be there in person, Mr Dolmetscher was fully authorised and empowered to speak on her behalf and perhaps a meeting between them would help to sort things out. Damian felt flattered and wooed and marvelled at the promptness of the invitation as he separated the enclosed return train-ticket from the paperclip.

Damian also appreciated the composition of the request; there were some nice turns of phrase and the tone was just right. Good paper too. He smiled. That was a classy gambit if ever there was one. The contents had been worthy of the envelope and he forgave the succinct addressing. He could see himself meeting Mr Dolmetscher, waving the letter around in one hand and saying, -

'You had me at "Dear Mister Email", Mr Dolmetscher.'

No. He would say:

'Pleased tameetcha Mr Doltmetscha, you had me at "Dear",' the letter waving in his hand, otherwise it wouldn't work. What he said had to be clearly linked to the contents of the letter, he didn't want any misunderstandings. Or he could say:

'Pleestameetcha, won't you guess my name?' and Mr Dolmetscher could reply:

'Mr Email, I presume!'

But wait, hang on. Hang on a minute. When was the

blinking appointment? Today at 2.30! It was today at 2.30!
There was plenty of time. It looked like he was going to be
active in location B after all. Damian checked where he had
to go on Google maps. It was quite close to the cathedral
and in an area of the city that was largely devoted to minor
local-government sub-offices and social service providers of
various types. You could get a holistic massage round the
corner. There was no point asking if they did 'extras', he
thought, if it was holistic. It was already all-in. All included.
All the massage you could take. If you asked they would say
'No we don't, the clue's in the name, dumbass,' then throw
you out into the street. Into the gutter. 'Scumbag!' Then slam
the door.

He could easily drive there or go on the scooter but the
Vespa was out of action until he sorted it, he'd have to do
something about it and would do. He had free train tickets,
the journey would make a change and the station was five
minutes away. Damian could see on the screen map that he
would have to go down Commercial Rd from the station to
get to the centre of town and this risked being a bit tedious
as he dimly recalled having to make short cuts through the
dullest of supermarket car-parks and then trudging up the long
uninspiring road when he'd gone there before. It took you to
a corner where you met the busy traffic on the internal ring-
road; you crossed and that was it. Was it half an hour on the
train, or maybe a bit less? Then what? Twenty minutes up the
road. Ok, there's plenty of time and plenty of trains. Factor in
some extra time for contingencies, just in case.

Damian thought he'd put a tie on and wear his green garb; it
would be basically an all-green look with dark shirt and yellow

tie. It was only the county town, the county city actually, not London, so he was sure he'd get away with it and besides, no one knew him there. He would need the shoes that made the great sound on the pavement. That was really walking. They sounded so amazing you felt that you had a job keeping up with yourself. The sound they made was subtle too, not your over-strident metal heel things, just a great sound from a purposeful stride. On wooden-floored footbridges they rang out phenomenally well. The tie? Maybe not the yellow one. It drew the eye too much for this and didn't go with the cool foot-fall, too flashy. There came a voice:

'May I suggest your grandfather's red and blue variegated tie sir? Appropriate neckwear for town, with a hint of "hommage", if I may say so sir.'

'Thank you, yes.'

8

The address he'd been given was part of a nineteenth-century terrace of three-storey buildings stretching down the street, all basically the same as each other, yet differing in small details.

Damian stood on the other side of the road and contemplated. Their brickwork had been covered in magnolia-coloured paint many times. Or was it actually cream? Or beige? Regulations seemed to dictate that this area of the city had to be mostly in that colour, whatever it was. Was there a specific name for it if you had to order some yourself? Could you have 2 litres of 'Urban off-white creamy magnolia rice-pudding no burnt bits beige', please?' Each painting event had laminated in a layer of dirt which wanted to bubble out in blisters and the latest grime was urgently needing covering over. Window ledges were spiked and netted to deter pigeons and seagulls but didn't seem to do much good as they were everywhere. The rear of city-centre high street shops built in the 60's and 70's abutted opposite and were similarly grimy but their paint scheme was slightly different, more white than cream; had their regulations been modernised to reflect post-war optimism? Updated, but with a nod to what had gone before?

His building was fronted with a long, frosted dirty window which supported a twelve-inch border of lead-lined coloured glass, mostly blue and red, all covered in road filth, at the top. Damian crossed to inspect the door and saw how the layers of paint had been worn away in parts to reveal a topographical cross-section through time like a Grand Canyon on a fractal scale. Variations of magnolia and cream dominated its upper levels but deeper down there were changes and you could see a light blue coat over a lighter green one and, here and there, directly below, the dark green of the original surface. It would make a good photograph he thought. He could call it 'Paintscape: East Street'.

A small polish-encrusted brass plaque by the door read "Royal Air Force Association" and just above, next to the bell, was a small plastic name-plate which said 'Local History Association'. He was thirty minutes early and about to wander off when the door opened and a boy, who looked to be aged between nine and thirteen, came out holding some books and a pencil case.

'Do you want to go in?' Damian didn't have time to answer. 'You can wait in there,' and the boy left him at the entrance and walked off down the street, leaving the door open.

Damian watched him getting further and further away and then looked through the doorway. He did want to go in, but not just yet because he liked hanging around. But he could go in and hang around inside, waiting, and waiting was something Damian didn't mind doing. Waiting was a kind of non-doing. Either way, in or out, he would be waiting. He would go in and wait inside. He entered a rather narrow hall which led to stairs straight ahead and had a door to the right half-way down, which was open, which he went into.

It was, or had been, a bar, as the bar was still there and behind it you could see ghostly shapes in the regulation beigey paint scheme where wall brackets had held bottles of spirits and left their imprints on the tobacco-stained walls. Small black holes showed where screws had been taken out. Framed paintings, or prints, were hung around the room depicting aircraft in flight. Across the top of the long window, was a stained-glass section which had 'Per ardua ad astra' written into a banner in the middle with R.A.F roundels at either end, set against red, clear and blue wavy panels in the shapes of billowing clouds about the size of his hand. There was a dark-brown carpet across most of the room and the shapes and colours of the original design were hard to make out, as though the once factory-fresh floor covering had been expertly camouflaged by time itself. Areas of linoleum showed where the carpet didn't reach and where he stood, at the threshold of the room, three layers of it had been worn through to reveal the denatured grey wood of the floorboards.

The building was silent with that strange and oppressive stillness that empty buildings have, and there was little noise from the street, the sound of occasional passing cars only seeming to deepen the echoing noiselessness. It had been a bar but it was a bar no more and Damian lamented its passing; it had been repurposed and there were clues, ones you might detect in a community 'hub' you see in some churches. There was a free-standing mobile book-carrier thing in the middle with a small handwritten sign saying 'Book Swap' on it, a large square low table in a corner with a couple of grey plastic chairs, six more stacked in a corner and some old shelving units with stuff in them in the other. There ought to be a sale of garden produce in plastic bags to set it off, he thought, with an honesty box.

Maybe it was a waiting room? Damian prided himself on

his waiting skills and was even sometimes annoyed that he hadn't managed to finish what he was doing whilst waiting, like reading something, when the time he was waiting for finally came, even after several hours. He approached the former bar to investigate a pile of magazines and found 'Positive News' which had been around for a while but was everywhere these days, another beneficiary of the new anti-anxiety times. He picked one up and went to a chair by the table, humming 'Babylon's Burning' by The Ruts to himself as he sat down, although he wasn't at all anxious. He had every right to be there.

On the table was a half-folded black and white contemporary facsimile of the local area's nineteenth-century Cassini map, and someone had been drawing on it. All the rivers and streams were picked out in blue felt pen and blue pencil crayon had been used to broaden the water features into marshy wetlands at various places. He could see that this map didn't make any distinction between main roads, by-roads, tracks or foot paths. They were all pretty much given equal weight with parallel black lines. Brown had been used to colour between these lines and Damian could see that the artist was linking up the different routes to find ways of getting around the map which avoided crossing the blue parts. That was clever, you could see the best way of travelling the area without getting your feet wet and so find the most ancient ways to get around. That was fascinating; he would get a map like that and do the same when he got home. Damian loved mapgazing and he examined it carefully.

'Mr Email?' shouted a voice eventually from up the stairs. 'Mr Email?'.

'Buggeramus!' Always just when you were getting into it. He folded the map as best he could and put it back on the table and the magazine went into his inside breast pocket. He stood up, moved forward, looked behind to make sure he hadn't left anything, engaged the purposeful stride, adapted for interior circumstances, departed the bar and went up the drab carpeted stairs to an off-white corridor with a same-coloured half-open door at the end which he decided to make for. Magnolia marshmallow cream beige was everywhere, the place shimmered with it. A couple of doors with numbers – sideshows – he wanted the main event. To the door, at the door. This wasn't a waiting room; this was an empty office, well that clearly wasn't his seat, so he'd sit on this one here and wait.

9

Damian was sitting in front of a large desk displaying some classic items; an old-school telephone with a dial, a three-tier in-out-pending wire baskety thing, a hefty blue-green onyx ashtray which could take a conference of six cigars at a time, a compact chrome device for cigarette ash, and a rotating carrousel of ink stamps. Facing him was a high-status leather and chrome swivel chair. There was a framed certificate on the wall and a filing cabinet by the door. Everything that could be black was black and it was all a bit too much for the modestly-sized room, making it feel cramped. Damian hadn't seen such an uncompromisingly officious office in a long, long time.

'We can do business here,' he thought and was about to rotate the stamps, and probably pick one out to see what it said, when there was the noise of a door opening in the corridor behind him.

'Mr Email!'' the speaker clearly knew where Damian was, as it was not the loud enquiry of before but more of a softening up; footsteps on the corridor were getting nearer. Another 'Mr Email!' and in came the host.

'Mr Email, I'm Harry-Dan.'

'Mr Dolmetscher, pleased to meet you, Damian.' The recent entrant came over to shake his hand then skirted the desk and sat down in front of him.

'Thank you so much for coming. Lorna is delighted.'

'That's alright, thanks for the train tickets.'

'Don't mention it! Oh dear, too late, you have. Well don't mention it again,' said the other with a forgiving smile.

He could sense that his interlocutor was something of a merry Andrew and felt uneasy, wondering why he'd thought of him as an 'interlocutor' and what exactly was a 'merry Andrew' anyway? Damian became wary.

'I was here a bit early and there was a boy...,'

'Don't mind him. Lorna is really so sorry,' the 'so' being emphasised.

'Please tell Lorna that it's really not a big deal I was just...,'

Dolmetscher deftly cut across and told how Lorna had been very upset when she'd got Damian's feedback and hoped that they could work something out, rescue something from the wreckage, as it were. Damian hadn't meant to hurt anybody's feelings and certainly hadn't wanted to cause any offence. No offence had been taken as such but, given the nature of the program, and Lorna's long-term interest in historical therapeutics, Lorna felt that a different approach was needed here and had asked that he, Dolmetscher, be a sort of go-between, an interlocutor on her behalf, if you will, to try and patch things up and would that be ok with Damian? Could they start again? And could Lorna invite him out for lunch?

'No, I'm alright thanks, I had a sandwich on the way,' was Damian's polite refusal which Harry-Dan declined, pointing out how it wouldn't make Lorna really, really happy, so it ended with a 'Yes that would be great.'

Dolmetscher skirted the desk again and led the way back out of the room and down to the street. Damian didn't like following people who knew where they were going and he didn't, but the pavement was too narrow to walk side by side so he had to follow, and keeping up wasn't easy, Harry-Dan's stride being purposeful-plus.

A short distance later and they'd reached the carriage entrance to what had been a coaching inn but was now a standard city-centre pub, also largely magnolia, but with some black-painted wooden half-timbering and some red-painted signs with gold gothic lettering in various places. It was a kind of alleyway used as an outside amenity for smokers: fringed with lean-to sheds, fire-escapes and small brick buildings, one of which emitted intermittent unpleasant grating whirr noises, and a handful of tables were dotted around here and there.

'This is my favourite place and I use it a lot when I'm in town. They know my ways here. One of my ways is to have lunch when the kitchen's closed. I don't do it on purpose to put them out, it's just that I prefer to start lunch after 2.30; it's somehow transgressive don't you think? My favourite table is right there, you sit yourself down and I'll sort things out at the bar. Chicken sandwiches ok for you? Lager ok? Damian had no time to answer, the other was gone inside and Damian made his way to the designated table. He was now suspicious. He could imagine the predictable lacklustre magnolia interior of the pub and this alleyway backyard amenity area was actually pretty crappy too.

Cigarette stubs and dog ends lay on the ground, the wall-mounted ashtray box by the main door was overflowing, the glass ashtrays on the tables were full as well, dog-ends drowned in tarry water – Damian could smell their sour tang without effort. Grimy soil-dirt filled the spaces between the bricky cobbles and sickly green stuff grew there. Looking around, Damian was not surprised to see an actual dog turd clogging a drain's cast-iron grill.

The table was one of those flat-pack wooden garden-centre semi-disposable ones which looked ancient and knackered after six-months use, being quite crappy in the first place. Its wood was grey, rotting in places and the heads of rusty nails showed. He checked the bench for nails and sat down. If there was a word to encapsulate what he felt about this place, that word was 'ordure', oh, and 'crappy'. Two words then.

His curiosity satisfied and soured, Damian took out 'Positive News' from his jacket, hoping for a lift, but he only had time to take in the headline:

'Uptight? Everything is alright!', turn to some book reviews on the back page:

'Feel-good fiction! – Thrilling new murder mystery serial!', (surely that was stretching the positive editorial policy a lot; it was an ill wind for sure) and:

'It's Yes!' – a self-improvement book telling you how to ask for, and get, what you wanted, (that was easy, Damian thought, just ask nicely, use the magic word) before Dolmetscher appeared at the doorway with two enormous-looking goblets of amber Belgian beer, each with a one-inch head.

Only strong Belgian beer ever looked like that, fretted Damian, and he groaned within. Belgians were used to it but Damian felt fearful. He didn't like the current iteration of lager: it all tasted of rice and syrup, had exotic names but was all made in the same factory in Burton-on Trent. Nobody seemed to know or care what 'authentic', meant anymore. Lager had been becoming spitefully strong and these beers, being Belgian, would be even stronger. Damian felt tired already, worried about the inevitable onslaught.

10

'Sandwiches coming in a minute,' Harry-Dan put the beers down carefully, swung a leg over his bench, then the other, and sat down.

'Help yourself.' Dolmetscher took out a tobacco tin from his pocket opened it, took himself a pinch and a cigarette paper and pushed it across to Damian, who did the same.

'Thanks.'

Dolmetscher picked up his glass, klinked Damian's with it, said 'cheers' and took an ample swig. Damian took his glass, the klink still perhaps ringing in the air, and swigged the same, although less. There was a sense that both men wanted to let out an 'ahhh…' and the moment seemed to require it, but it didn't happen and they set to rolling their cigarettes. There was a silence which Damian broke.

'Mr Dolmetscher, I don't want to…,'

'Harry-Dan please, or H-D if you like. I'm proud of my name and I like the courtesy of 'Mister' but there is, with it, a formality ill at odds with our surroundings, and my mission.'

'Wow!' thought Damian, this beer is good. It's damn good.

'Ok Harry-Dan, call me Damian.'

'Thanks Damian.'

'Cheers again Harry-Dan.' and Damian klinked his glass against the other's and took it back to his lips for another slurp. There came a warmth, a relaxation, a settling-in; the rank tang of hitherto was displaced by a better odour. He loved that new smell. It smelt like…, it smelt like…, like bonhomie. Bonhomie in the afternoon.

'So what was it about Lorna that set you off?'

'I really respect her. It was only what she said at the end.'

'What was that?'

'Go for gold! Excel and only connect.'

'Oh that, they all say that. They have to. It's sort of contractual.'

'What do you mean?'

'Well ok, not contractual 'per se', more a code, a kind of 'vade mecum'. Damian had heard the Latin term before, quite frequently at one point, but had never looked it up and didn't know what it meant. It was odd to use it, he thought, a bit show-pony. It smelt of the lamp, like 'ceteris paribus'. He vowed to leave it undiscovered in case he started to use it himself.

'A code?'

'Yes, "Only connect" is used a lot these days but most people don't really get it. You probably know that its origin is usually given as being from E.M. Forster's "Howard's End", chapter 22, where it's actually more of an apologia than an exhortation but generally nowadays it just means "join-the-dots" with no greater significance than that. It's a bit trite. Correction. It is trite. We use it as a code.'

'A code?'

'Yes, code for "Use Wikipedia a lot", i.e mainly use Wikipedia, and "Excel!" means "Mainly use Excel spreadsheets a lot", and "Go for gold!" means "Aim high!".'

'How is one supposed to know the code?' Damian was careful to avoid ambiguity.

'I know. It's mysterious. Most people just take it at face

value. It does no harm. In fact, the last one, "Go for gold!",
was put in by the marketing people who wanted a slogan
with three elements because those are the only ones allowed
nowadays apparently. I thought it weak and demurred during
the consultation period but I think I can see their point:
"Only connect! Excel!" is a tad too strident and does need
balancing. I suggested "Concretise!" which I liked a lot, but
they said it wasn't obvious enough, so I thought we could
compromise with "Make it real!" which would have done the
job better, I think, but they wouldn't go for it, so there it is,
"Go for gold!" meaning "Aim high!".

Harry-Dan went into a further lengthy explanation of the
slogan so that Damian would completely understand why he
needn't be needled by it, explaining that, right at the beginning,
he had wanted to find a discrete set of words that would
describe a particular instance, but couldn't:

'That instance being, for example, when you are walking
along a pebbly beach, you with some friends, and you see
a distant marker, such as a post or something, and you
pick up a stone and you say to your companions "See that
distant marker!" and they look at it. You throw the stone
at it. Amazing! You hit it! They say "Do that again!" You say
nothing, a fleeting faraway look betokening deep knowledge
and wonderful skill is all that is needed at this moment. They
say "Lucky!" You say "Lucky? That's what I was trying to do".
Actually, best not to say anything and let the look do the
heavy-lifting, but we couldn't find the right words and the "Go
for gold!" versus "Make it real!" contest began, "Go for gold!"
coming out on top.

Both glasses had been fully emptied for a few minutes

already and tidemarks of suds languished down their sides, hinting at the passage of time. 'Blimey!' thought Damian, that had gone down quick and he hadn't even lit his first cigarette. The barman brought two more foam-topped beers, unsummoned. Damian lit up. Damn, that was great tobacco.

'Using Wikipedia, that's obvious but what's Excel?'

'It's a program mostly used by accountants, I think. It's the new version of accountancy paper, do you remember it? I don't know if you can get it anymore.'

'Maybe in America?' suggested Damian.

'We use it to arrange our information,' he explained, 'like a notepad. It saves using paper, which is a godsend, no more bulging briefcases, clutter and all that, it's really much easier and you can add new bits, and give them names and use text boxes. It can sometimes be a bit too clever and you can forget why you wrote something, and forget what you called it, or make too many copies of something and have multiple files flying around but basically its very helpful. It helps make things clear, it helps you think.'

The barman returned with two chicken sandwiches. Damian had found his appetite again and Harry-Dan wasted no time getting stuck into his one. Damian appreciated the sandwich; it was so chickeny. Where could you get chicken like that these days? Oh nice touch, there was mayonnaise with tarragon in it. Damn, that was a great sandwich. Damian wanted to walk up and down on the battlements playing a sad Scottish song, a pibroch for its passing, on the bagpipes but managed to re-focus on the present moment, rolling himself another cigarette from his own packet.

'So Damian, could we have another chance, yes?'

'Yes, sure, let's do it. With Lorna?'

'Yes, she'll be the over-all supervisor but I'll take operational command, if that's ok?'

'That's fine with me,' Damian said, all his qualms having been escorted off the premises en masse and told not to bother coming back and there flowed conversation, beer and cigarettes.

Lorna Dune wasn't really her real name. Lorna was her real first name but she'd changed her surname just before going to university, after coming back from a gap-year stay on a vineyard in Australia where her original last name had attracted unwelcome attention, so she'd decided to change it, it being otherwise an old one and worthy of respect in any case. H-D would not say what it was. Was it maybe something like 'Spearshank?' asked Damian, before carrying on with a list of possible uncomfortable names. Harry-Dan gave in like a good sport. It had been 'Dunny' which didn't sound right in Australia. Of course it had. Damian winced, he should have, could have, got there first.

Damian shed his bourgeois inhibitions and opened up, telling Harry-Dan how his own name had become somewhat of a pain in the albatross but he wouldn't change it, although it was definitely difficult sometimes. When he'd been younger, at school, it had sounded a bit exotic like 'Émile', even a bit glamourous; 'E-mail' like 'He-man'. Nobody had invented email at that time and nobody had paid it any attention at university either but then suddenly it had become a millstone.

Actually, he was proud of it. It meant something like 'enamel' in French, maybe went back to gothic. 'To email' or 'émailler' meant 'to fill in with enamel'. Our word 'melt' had the same

root, think 'schmelzen' in German, or 'Schmalz'. In fact, the
'mail' in 'email', the messaging service, actually comes from
old-english 'male' meaning small travelling bag, like a diplomatic
bag, related to modern French 'malle', a kind of suitcase, did
he see what he meant? 'Email' and 'Email' were superficially
the same, but different. He did see what he meant. They were
homonymic and homophonic but different meanic.

Harry-Dan's name was Central-European and meant
something like 'interlocutor', a bit more than a translator
maybe, someone who could fill stuff in, maybe they were the
same words 'Email' and 'Dolmetscher', though both silently
decided that this seeking-after-synthesis felt far-fetched
and moved on. They shared secrets and opinions. Damian
showcased his 'take' on British lager-beer and H-D felt exactly
the same about it.

'You know, there used to be an American beer they said
tasted like piss, but now they all do.'

'Actually, I disagree, if they actually had piss in they'd taste
better' said the other.

Both had seen that bit in the documentary about Richard
III's excavation in the Leicester car park. The passionate
seeker of Richard's resting place was standing above the
resultant hole and in it were two archaeologists wearing full-
body disposable protective clothing.

'Is that him? Is that really him?' cried out Richard's dogged
bounty hunter, thrilled, 'Is that really him?' Her lifetimes'
ambition was being made flesh. Correction, surely a lifetime's
ambition was being made bone? They laughed.

'Sorry, carry on.'

'Oh! Is that a wound?' The camera had zoomed in to

show a diamond-shaped half-inch hole in the dome of a skull protruding from the earth. The camera pulled back to show the two pick-axe-carrying professionals who confessed their error. One of them had bashed it.

Some debate ensued. Were they both carrying pick-axes? Were their tools actually, in fact, 'mattocks', rather than 'pick-axes', as such? Had they been wearing hard-hats? Was it more like an inch-wide hole in the skull? But no matter. They'd both seen it on the television that one time only but you couldn't see it on Youtube now, could you? Was it a cover-up? A conspiracy?

They talked of history more. This island story, who's kidding who? Never invaded since 1066? What about Prince Louis of France, could've got himself crowned in Westminster Abbey if the Pope had gone for it, with full backing of the barons for sure, well most of them.

What about William of Orange's invasion? 463 ships and 40,000 men with a march right across England from Torbay to London. You didn't hear that talked about much, did you?

Another thing, Jack of Kent' the folkloric bogeyman of Monmouthshire is actually John of Gaunt. Yes, there was a pub called that down the road from Gaunt's castle in Grosmont, where Damian's parents had lived. Did the other one know that the owner of the castle before Gaunt was an Earl of Kent, amongst other titles, or something like that; so it was like a mix-up of the two.

Was King Arthur a similar mix-up? Isn't the welsh for emperor 'amirardur' or something like that? 'Ymerawdwyr' corrected the other − that did sounded a bit like 'Arthur' if you said it properly, or pronounced it wrongly.

Tolkein had nicked Sam Gamgee from Sam the dog in 'Niall's Saga' and Gandalf from the Volvo legends. Correction 'Völva'. Damian shared his secret about the Loch Ness monster, swearing the other to secrecy, who so swore. 'That's dynamite, I won't tell a soul,' and they shared the secret of the skeleton found down the well in the cellar under a shop, which had been an inn, under two huge pieces of broken rococo frieze, which had been hushed up, but they got the stone out and you can see it in the garden.

They both knew that 'Nando's' was originally the name of one of the first seventeenth-century coffee houses in London. And so it went on, and enjoyably on, two insiders holding forth, debating the petty points, having a great time.

11

Damian's soul was being stirred in the pleasantest way possible but shouldn't there also be a darker, wistful blue note to contrast with the conviviality and so set it off, like diamonds on a black cloth. A mournful ballad comes at the end of the band's audience-pleasing set and the noisy crowd falls silent as a clear voice sings out a timeless story, all eyes a-glitter, moved by the music to shine. That time had come for Damian. The time for righteous melancholy was here and now Damian reached, wanting to share it.

'I love history Harry-Dan, I really love it, really love it.'

'Of course you do, we all do.'

'No, I really do.'

'Yes we do, we all do.'

'But I really love it, but…, but…,'

Harry-Dan would have said 'Spit it out man!' at this point but as he'd already used the expression twice before with Damian and this didn't feel like the right time to say it again.

'What is it?'

'It's…, It's…,'

'Yes?'

'It's that…, that…,'

'Go on.'

'It's that sometimes I just don't get it.'

'How do you mean?'

'I read a book about something and when I'm finished, I don't remember anything. Anything important. It's like I have to read it all over again. And again. What they say doesn't sink in.'

'Like which book?'

'Any of them. All of them.'

'Can you give me an example to work with?'

'I can't remember...,' a pause, he remembered one, 'like a book about Magna Carta I got once, it was great, really well done, you couldn't get a better one about Magna Carta. But all I could remember at the end was King John's phenomenal movements.'

'That's a bizarre detail, I'll admit.'

'Yes I know, he moved his entire court an average of 12.5 miles per day over his sixteen-year reign. He was in one place for a stay of a week or more for only 13% of his time. He was on the move the whole time. And he was cruel – he killed someone in a tower in Rouen and he starved a mother and child to death. He gave them a sheaf of corn and a rasher of bacon then locked them up. That was in Corfe I think.'

'Well that's quite a lot of detail.'

Damian was being frank and open but not completely so. He didn't mention his foibles; he didn't mention that the more he liked a book, the less likely he was to finish it. Finished, they would've been 'read' and somehow over. To read three-quarters of it and then to start reading it again from the beginning another time was his modus operandi. Some of his all-time favourite books had hardly been read at all; he'd give himself a one-page treat, then put it away and start on another one. His absolutely best book was being kept to read sometime in retirement, maybe just before the end.

'And another thing, I like visiting castles, I love visiting them and I always get the guidebook but I hate them.'

'You hate castles?'

'No, it's the guide books. You've either got to be an architect or a kid to get something out of them but the castles are just as bad in a way. I see the bare walls and can't imagine anything having been there. I used to..., you know..., for a joke ...., on the way in..., go to the walls and..., and put my hands on them and do that "If only the stones could talk" thing. It was funny, but wasn't really. I wanted them to talk but they said nothing to me. Don't I have the right imagination? And the books...,'

'You talked about the guide books.'

'No, I mean books about history, the books are annoying as well. It's like they're stupid stories made up to conform to other stupid stories. They repeat things people have said before. Where's the truth? They blabber away and prove things with idiotic facts. You can prove anything with a fact, so what? What's the real story? I don't get the real story in history. It's people making up stories and calling that history.'

Had Damian been a better and more complete man, he would have now burst into tears, be relieved of a burden, and be ready for counselling, but it was too late now for such honesty.

'I'm afraid we don't have a cure for Email syndrome Mr Email.' H-D loved using that line at a time like this and it was never to be resisted; it was sometimes even helpful. The crisis was before him and a firework display was now called for.

'It's strange how we often have to use exotic words to describe this kind of thing, like "ennui" or "angst" or "mal de siècle" or "malaise" or "zeitgeist" don't you think?'

'Zeitgeist?' Damian had fallen for It.

'Well maybe not "Zeitgeist", but if we give what you've got a name, you'll hang on to it and never be free so let's try not do that. I quite understand what you are going through and have seen it myself many times. You are "something". I was "something" myself, yes, I was "it" once myself.'

'What were you?'

'What I was is not important. It's what you are that is?'

'What am I?'

'Shall we give it a name then?'

'Yes.'

'You are blocked.'

'Blocked?'

'You are blocked, it seems to me, in two important ways, you are blocked from within and from without.' Damian was attentive and inattentive, and couldn't help wondering if Harry-Dan would use 'outwith': a term used by official spokespeople in Scottish news reports which was gaining traction in England. Harry-Dan noticed and wanted to snap his fingers at Damian but settled for an effective rhetorical pause and an appropriate look.

'Your forward progress is impeded by a "bloquage" and you are internally "bloqué". One of these blockades is you and the other represents circumstances outwith yourself.' Damian perked up. Harry-Dan went into his tried and tested digression therapy which Damian tuned into and out of as he considered how he was blocked and what was blocking him.

'…and for many years they believed, maybe coming from Galen or before, they believed that the body was ruled by humours, which had to be very carefully watched. People were very fussy about eating, you'd be surprised. It was basically their only medicine. What I mean is that eating was the only treatment they had which worked, which helped them. So eating was carefully thought about, you know. They thought that cooking carried on in the stomach, so you had to eat things in the right order because if you got things mixed up in your stomach it wouldn't work properly and would start to go off and decay which would block you, and stink you up.

They were actually quite modern in their fussy ways. You needed hot and dry things to open up your workings which was called an "aperitif" from the latin "aprire" to open. You'd open up with sweeties called "confections" which were sweet and spicy, think: cumin, aniseed, ginger, caraway, fennel and sweetened milky drinks, and wine of course. That would open you up. And vinegar. This all opens up the gubbins.

Next comes the easy-eating stuff like fruit, after that your lighter vegetables, lettuce, parsley and light meat like chicken, also broth or pottage at this stage. We come now to the heavy stuff; beef and pork. Last are pears and nuts and then you finish off the process with a digestive course. This is the most important one; aged cheese and/or another kind of spicy sweetmeat and/or a spicy wine called "hypocras" was recommended.

The word "digest" actually comes from the Latin as well and refers directly to the compartmentalisation inherent in this sequencing. "To digest" basically, or literally, means "to compartmentalise". There's a lot of that old-thinking still around. In fact, in a way, it's all basically still around.'

12

'Being blocked, that's hard to digest.' Damian had nodded along to the monologue and now felt like compartmentalising it.

'Hang on Damian, don't get all pessimistic on me now. You were the one who told me you were blocked in the first place. You told me yourself that you were blocked everywhere and now I see that you are loosening up. I think we need to sharpen our pencils. Excuse me will you, I'll go and get them.' He swung himself out of the bench and went off to the bar.

Damian didn't feel especially blocked, just himself, and was enjoying the beery fumes working their magic in his digestion. Beer first to open up and then more beer on top, then chicken, white bread, tarragon, a little mayonnaise, followed by beer and then more beer, wonderful. The dismal surroundings didn't seem so tawdry now; you could imagine townsmen and women all quaffing merrily together, cigarette butts raining to the ground, a faithful wee doggy stirs from beneath its master's table to find a quiet out-of-the-way corner to unblock itself, and then returns for a treat and a cuddling fuss.

The dirty cobbles, he noticed, were actually nineteenth-century originals, dimpled to make it easier to clear up after horses and there was even a ring on the wall to tether them to; the clip-clopping and jangling, the whinnying and neighing, the smell of saddle soap and dubbin, were almost palpable. Maybe he would bring his daughter here when she came for her annual visit, her husband might appreciate the gritty authenticity. H-D came back out with a half-pint mug in each hand.

'Here's our hypocras! We've got to wrap things up a bit. I've got some stuff to take care of back at the ranch.'

'By the way, what's the connection of your history association with the R.A.F.?'

'Very interesting point,' which Harry-Dan was happy to elaborate, 'because the history association is itself lodged in history. Our building was a Royal Air Force Association club house, originally for world war II veterans, and then part of a network of clubs round the country for ex-members of the Royal Air Force but the old soldiers have marched into history and century 21 has sadly had to carry on without them. The council owns it but nobody wants to be the one to erase them completely, so it hasn't really been touched or done up. Will be one day, I'm sure. Pleased to talk about it but in the meantime, behold these beauties!' Harry-Dan waved the two glasses around invitingly 'Here's the only 'digestif" that really works. Word to the wise: we'll go over a few things, quickly recap, and then let these two seal the deal.'

'Ok let's do it, but what are those drinks?'

'Cider and gin cocktails invented by a certain Mr Hubert Butt of Somersetshire. It's cider with a measure of gin in. Can you guess the name?'

'Is it called a Hubert?'

'No, it's named after where he lived.'

'A Somersetshire?'

'No, he was briefly living in Worcestershire when he came up with it.' Damian pondered. There came a revelation.

'A Bertie Wooster then!'

'No.' Damian refined his revelation, expecting to hole it in one.

'A Hubertie Wooster!'

'No, he was living in Worcestershire but his drink is called after the name of his house.'

'Hubert's Hole?' Damian was getting desperate.

'No, Butts Bank,' Damian vowed to check this later, 'but before we give them our full attention, let's clarify some specifics. Is everything alright right now?'

'Yes, it's all good, I really enjoyed myself.'

'That's great. Are you ok with Lorna?'

'Yeah, totally, thank her will you, again, for the vicarious hospitality.'

'Was that you being a tad sarcastic Damian?' Had Damian caused offence again, by accident?

'No, not at all, I was just trying to unblock myself a bit by stretching my vocabulary. What I meant was, although I am admittedly disappointed that she couldn't be here in person, her appointed agent has fully represented her in a way that she, I'm sure, were she here, would be entirely in accord therewith.' H-D nodded.

'And she can supervise your E.P.Q with myself as your immediate sub-supervisor, both you and I being, as it were, under her overarching supervision?'

'For sure, yes.'

'And that you will, and in due course, find yourself a subject for the said E.P.Q?'

'I will so duly perform.'

'I think that's it then.'

'Do I need to sign anything?'

'No.'

'How do we keep in touch?'

'Have a guess. Let's drink to your E.P.Q. We won't call it that anymore, too dull, think of a code-word and tell me what it is some time.'

'In code?'

'No, in clear, and, if I were you, take my advice, try and get yourself to the station pretty sharpish.' H-D stood up and raised his glass.

'Henceforward!' Damian did the same.

'Henceforward!' and they klinked their glasses together with gusto.

Damian was expecting it to be revolting. He'd gone off cider because of the sulphites and gin made his neck swell, but this! It was neither cider nor gin but a magical potion of junipery deliciousness. Gulp, gulp, gulp and it was gone. If that was a Butts Bank, it was a damn good one.

He found himself at the pedestrian crossing, on his way to the station, waiting for the chance to get over the traffic and head back down Commercial Rd. Yes, it had been a transgressive afternoon, perhaps too transgressive with everybody going about their business all around and being normal. Damian's head was transcendent and the universe was a bit distorted; it felt like it was maybe a parallel one.

The thing would be to look normal so as not to get noticed and try not to bump into anything on the way. The purposeful stride would not be engaged as he might not have time to take in things properly before he tripped over them. He'd use the 'I'm invisible' walk down the middle of the pavement, which allowed for the option of going left or right, out of the way of things that got in the way, as and when events dictated, and he would remember to breath normally. And he wouldn't get into a fracas, or any kind of altercation, never mind what anyone said, whatever the circumstances.

Damian couldn't choose whether to sit on the one, almost-vacant bench on the platform or to lean carelessly against something upright. Perhaps he could pull out his 'Positive News' from his pocket as a decoy, but then he might fumble or drop it and have to try and pick it up again. He would leave it be for the moment. Maybe a walk up the platform, but then there was a risk that he might end up walking in circles and attract attention but, no matter, deep joy, the train was here. Careful now: wait…, wait…, wait…, come on doors, come on, pshhhhtt, don't rush! In, go left, take the first one, sit, breath out.

What an afternoon, what time was it now? It was much later than he'd thought. What a damn fine afternoon.

He conjured up the image of Harry-Dan to fix him in his mind's eye before the forgetting was too advanced. The clothes he wore were dark. Were they mostly off-black, very dark grey or extremely dark blue? Black magnolia? Black cream? Off-black dark clothes. The clothes were rumpled but smart. Rumpled, dark, but still smart like Isambard Kingdom Brunel's, but without the top hat. A tie? Surely there had been one but maybe not. Had there even been a discreet leather waistcoat? Damian thought so, but it was certainly unobtrusive.

Harry-Dan definitely had a pony-tail but it was easy to miss and sort of blended in with his clothes. Opposite the pony-tail he wore some kind of glassy pendant, or plastic semi-see-through thing, worn on a what? A thong? A string? His hair was black, but not black-black, there was grey in it, long individual grey strands. Were they bluey-grey strands? Was his hair grey then? It had seemed mostly..., mostly..., mostly grey, ...and black at the same time. Maybe bluey-greyey-black hair.

Damian didn't like describing people but he was ok with clothes and hair. He tried extending himself; Dolmetscher was pale-skinned but there was some colour in it, some ruddiness, lips were quite red and he was quite well-built, but not tall. Burly? Podgy? Were his hands podgy? Or small, but not podgy? He didn't talk loudly, almost murmuring, so was he quietly spoken? Did he have a bit of a northern accent? He definitely looked like a roadie. A roadie in his Sunday best without a rock tee-shirt on. A roadie at a wedding more like. Be alert! Be alert for the station.

The train had stopped. This wasn't his stop but it was getting nearer. He'd get up now and stand by the door, ready for the next one. Here it is, so out you get.

Damian felt able to deploy the purposeful stride to full effect and ride it all the way home. His foot slipped off the edge of the pavement into the gutter just once but the paving slabs here were a bit uneven and the council could be blamed for that one, not the stride. He wasn't being reckless, just normal and purposeful.

Back in his room at Epsilon Precinct, the door shut, he reminisced about what a great afternoon and early evening it had turned out to be and felt elation. There was some left-over chicken, some old baguette, some beer, but they were pale shadows and he'd had enough anyway. Just a cup of tea and 'Starship Troopers'.

He watched it until the bit where someone says 'What's your malfunction?' and laughed because he knew what his malfunction was and it wasn't even a malfunction. He was blocked and he was ok with that. There were ways to deal with blockages but a malfunction was more serious. You could end up having to replace the whole thing or spending lots of money trying to find what was wrong by a process of elimination. He was lucky because he was just blocked. He had to loosen-up and find a way around, flow like water …, flow like a river …, flow river flow…, Damian shut down and turned in.

He woke at just before four and went to the window, drew back the curtain and looked out to see the sky already lightening. There was bird song and he opened the window to hear it better. It was like a jungle out there, loud and noisy.

Some songs he recognised: 'fi ga ro, fi ga ro' and 'la cu ca ra cha, la cu ca ra cha', others made a rich soundscape of chitterings, whoops and bawdy trills. He went outside. The sounds came from everywhere but he couldn't see the birds; their voices must carry a long way and all meet up here in a soundscape tangle. He was alert. He was joyful. He knew this one would be perfect.

'Sorry about yesterday; I'll try and beat you to it this time,' and he got a move on to get down to the gate.

13

'Open a dossier,' was Damian's first thought when having
to begin thinking about something and that dossier always
needed a name, which could be as far as it ever got, named but
empty. 'Damian's Institute of Enquiry', could it be that? This
enquiry was going to be one of the biggest things he'd done
and would have to be massive, like a post-modern Corbusier-
Bauhaus institute of concrete, stone, glass and steel, standing
on a hill under the Californian sun, with its name chiselled into
it in huge letters visible from afar. No, the acronym would be
too off-putting. He'd have to think of another name to cut
into the white stone.

There had been a huge worked stone, part of an arrow-slit
from Grosmont castle, in his parents' garden and he'd had
to take it away when his mum had moved house. He'd been
able to do it but it hadn't been easy; his whole body had got
hot all at once as if lifting it had disturbed an energy, a passive
energy of heaviness and mass that had been locked in the
stone and it had passed into to him; he'd been relieved not
to have done himself some damage. Although the stone had
been hard to lift, it could be rolled quite easily and if he rested
it on one of its corners it could even be spun around under
his complete control, as if it weighed nothing. He'd always
thought of it as John of Gaunt's stone. That would be as good
a name as any, so codename 'Gaunt' it would be and it would
look appropriately gaunt in 6-foot high incised lettering on his
building, above the entrance.

The dossier now had a name and that was certainly a step in the right direction so he emailed Harry-Dan accordingly and succinctly thus;

Subject: Codename.

Content: 'Gaunt'.

Best regards Damian Email.

Nearly two weeks of diligent endeavour passed and no detail was too insignificant to record, and there were plenty of them. He didn't know exactly what he would choose to do for his enquiry, only that the project was called Gaunt and would be something to do with late-medieval history. He didn't know what he would need so he got it all, ripped from Wikipedia and put it in Excel, like Lorna said, and it worked well. It was time to stand back and taste the rough and ready home-brew he'd made but something was missing, or he'd missed something, and he went back inside Gaunt to make a second batch.

Damian, ever the optimist, liked to look on the bright side, whilst there was one, and this tasted a bit better, not fit for human consumption yet, but better than the first lot. It wasn't right to just spit it out and start again. He'd have to work harder, analyse, taste what was there and get a handle on it, figure out where to go from here. He needed to see more clearly and imaginated something up to help.

A winery in a new vineyard with everything against it: wrong soil, wrong climate, maybe wrong grape variety, but could the master winemaker turn this improbable set-up into a sought-after vintage? What were the first indications? He saw himself opening a tap in the stainless steel vat and pouring some of the contents into a small disposable plastic beaker and tasting it.

First on the mouth; barons, lots of barons, they wouldn't be told, that was King John and Henry III and it soon faded away; no barons seemed to suffer overmuch for their rebellious misconduct.

Then another flavour, a strong one; Edward I distracts the mightiest barons with his welsh wars, clever move that, and he doesn't stop there, he carries on into Scotland and bullies his way around. Sourness now; he kills the English Jews to get their money to pay his soldiers and build his castles, that's an unmistakeable unpleasantness.

What next? Some astringency; his son doesn't have his killer instinct and warrior credentials, there's a baronial bounce-back, this time with beheadings, and Edward II reaps the whirlwind.

Next, dominant and impossible to ignore: cherry, licorice and peppery notes – Edward III comes in with his 50-year reign. It's quite pleasant at first; his son accidently wins some big battles in France and the big barons are distracted by fighting and chivalry, but it's lacking balance at the end (there's Black Death everywhere), his son and heir dies and Edward is going senile. It's over.

His grandson doesn't have his reputation and some barons bite back. One of them rushes in to take the throne – that's bitter, vinegary – and Henry the Fourth is king. Then comes his son, wee vainglorious Henry V, who begets the wee-est Henry VI and it tails off into the Wars of the Roses: a lingering, cloying finish on the palate which stains your mouth red.

Damian checked back over his tasting notes. Digressions and side tracks had been becoming prominent lately, they were all worthy, interesting and possibly relevant but something was going wrong. He'd invested time and energy and been self-disciplined and got a grip on himself but it was starting to not make sense.

He had pillaged the internet like a fight-starved Viking hot for gold and been shamelessly robbing Wikipedia, stripping the dead and wounded of anything worth keeping and not giving a toss about them – well sometimes a drink of water, but usually nothing. He was hard-bitten, contemptuous and was as good as any of them, but the more he hoarded, the less he felt he had. His digital rampage had been fun. He had enjoyed himself but the goblet of sweet soomaky mead had taken on a doomaky taint.

Had the best of the fruit been gathered in already? Was he just chucking everything into the basket and not checking for blemishes anymore? What was he trying to make? A fine, distinguished and rare 'Premier Cru', a good ordinary 'Vin du Pays' or chutney? A premium chutney probably, like that apricot and ginger one from Yorkshire, it was great, but it was still just chutney. Damian did not want to be a premium chutney maker. He wanted to make a life-changing hypocras to be served at the top table, let those lower down the pecking order sooth their digestions with chutney. He was just trudging up and down the dusty rows of vines, without a hat and sweating under the sun and putting everything into his basket. Had he reached his level of competence and would never escape the drudgery? Damian wanted to be somewhere else, sitting on a sunny terrace with a sea view, under a parasol, toasting his success with Lorna and Harry-Dan over Butts Bank hypocrastic digestif cocktails.

Transferring his incipient frustrations onto others and

blaming them for his own inadequacies was not Damian's way of dealing with things but he did it nevertheless, subconsciously, not being able to help himself and Harry-Dan Dolmetscher began to take a battering.

What did the way he looked say about him? That pony-tail! Was he a bloody weekend pagan who called himself Uther Pendragon? What a hypocrite! Uther Pendragon? The father of King Arthur? A pagan? A bloody pagan? Dumbass! A hypocrite more like. One internet ferreting expedition had lead him to Tolkein again and now the 'Phial of Galadriel' was being offered for sale every time he went on his laptop, the result of an innocent click. Dumbasses! What was Dolmetscher doing wearing a fake elven princess's perfume bottle on a string round his neck? Was he a phoney?

Damian had read 'Catcher in the Rye' late in life and thought it poor. It was self-righteous solipsism. Solipsism writ-large. Solipsism writ-large with knobs on, standing on stilts made of gold. Was Dolmetscher really all that? Was he the big 'I am'? Or was he a phoney, just a hustler hassling him to make a sale on a commission-only basis? Damian wanted it to come together, but it wasn't; it was coming apart, and he knew he had to see his supervisor, despite, and because of, his misgivings.

14

A quick game of Email tennis ended conclusively with an H-D smash. Harry-Dan would come to him this time and would be in Damian's local pub for a transgressive afternoon working-session at 15.30 that afternoon, which suited Damian very well indeed and he turned up there ten minutes early for the appointment, fully recovered from his earlier dourness, got a drink and bagged the two of them a table outside.

It was his favourite pub and Damian was convinced it was probably one of the best in the country. It was great inside, but better out, as you could smoke, and was the perfected ideal of a 'gemütlich' beer garden, incarnating as it did, the quintessence of sociability. Damian was familiar with the foundation myth, known only to a few, which gave out that the present landlord had been obliged to ban 96 people when he took over some years ago; it had been an epic battle for gemütlichkeit – one against 96! That was heroic and worthy of a Siegfried, or an Arthur. No. Arthur couldn't hold the Saxons back. No, he was more like…, like…, like Garibaldi. Maybe the number of banned boozers had been exaggerated and the story embellished with the telling.

'Damian!' shouted Harry-Dan, appearing from the door to the pub bang on time, pint of beer in hand and coming over.

'Harry-Dan!'

'This is a nice spot. What's that you've got?'

'It's my favourite beer, Otter bitter, 3.6%.'

'The kindliest of session ales, I think I've got the same, we won't be booming and zooming like that last time with these.'

'That last time was great, I felt fine.'

'How's Gaunt going?' Dolmetscher got straight to the point and listened carefully, nodded frequently and asked useful questions as Damian described his methodology and his labours. 'Damian, that's great. You've really got stuck into the period but don't we still have a problem? Perhaps I should say, an opportunity?'

'An opportunity?'

'To decide what your enquiry is about. You've got the codename and that's a great start, but we need to find...,' Harry-Dan speech-marking with his fingers, 'a "thing" for you to get your teeth into: the subject no less.'

'Yeah I know, I don't really see it yet. I looked at a few things but thought, you know, so what?'

'I'm really happy about that. You've done all the boring bits and now you're looking for the good bits and that's the opportunity.' Damian was ready to be upbraided for not reducing the scope of his enquiry and, expecting that, wasn't expecting to be told that he was on the very threshold of it. Harry-Dan carried on in a similar upbeat way as the beers came and went using metaphors, allegories, and all manner of symbolic paraphernalia: boots, maps, compasses, cross-roads, even waterproof raincoats, to try and help Damian explore and develop his historical understanding. Maybe Damian was closer to discovering what he wanted to do than he realised? Anyway, it was all well on the way, he was sure. H-D went through some of the enquiries that had been done before:

'There's been: "Pea soup and Pottage v Barley and Broth", which was a comparative evaluation of low-status diets in

England and Scotland, "The Peasant as Other", speaks for itself, "Bondsmen and Beadsmen – two sides, same coin?", as above, "Palfreys and Paternosters – pilgrim's way?", same.'

Damian suggested: 'Apertures as Artefacts' on arrow-slits and got worked up about it for a minute or two, but left it as being too technical, and they moved on. Damian shared his qualms about the work he was doing but Harry-Dan didn't seem to be worried and Damian wasn't being feckless and unfocussed at all.

What was important was that at some point something would rush at him and say 'Pick me! Pick me!' and that would be the start of it, everything would tumble into shape and some tips were offered; Damian could do with loosening up, loosening up his thinking, he needed to forget about history and the facts and the dates and find the story, the real story. Facts got in the way of the truth. He needed do the opposite of what was conventional, what everybody was doing in the same way and find a new way, his way.

Damian liked this 'street' historical talk and gave as good as he got. He didn't like all the facts in history, they didn't seem to help much, many of them weren't even facts, not facts like in Maths, more like guesses or inventions, dressed up to look like them. History stories rehashed the same stuff over and over, most of it was actually just put together to make a believable story. You could bend it any way you wanted to. Damian liked a good historical reference book and the older books read well but the more modern ones were all pretending to be true, pretending to be scientists, or Marxists, or both.

'Marxists have their place,' cautioned Harry-Dan, needing to divert Damian from his antipathy to academics and he chose the nature of words as being a suitable topic:

'I am something of an amateur semiotician in my spare time, or should that be semioticist?'

'Is it a "seismatic?"' Damian had got to calling semiotics "seismatics" for a forgotten reason.

'That sounds like it could be right but I'm sure it isn't.' H-D looked it up on his smartphone, 'It's actually "semiotician", you're thinking of "semanticist" I think, which is different.'

They wouldn't split hairs about it and Damian felt half-right about it, wrongly.

'That's the problem with amateurs, they can be sloppy over the details, professionals can't afford to be woolly,' goaded Harry-Dan playfully, and he went on to talk about his love of words and the sounds they made.

Seems they rarely meant anything really; they were basically just the right sounds in the right order and if you got that then you had a coherent argument. Damian had a theory about English, that it had collected too many words from outside to mean things and so most didn't mean much, and offered some for scrutiny, which he felt to be dull as soon as they came out of his mouth. Harry-Dan came up with other more florid and persuasive examples which Damian hoped he would be able to remember and use later.

'And Damian, don't be afraid to use the language, get those words working for you, because it's the ideas that count, not the words but you'll find it pretty hard bringing them to life without the right words. Remember, you're not doing homework for school here, it's not going to be marked and given back to you with red pen all over it. It's your thing, for you, yourself.' and a few seconds of silence allowed the dust-cloud of gravitas to settle.

'Any other business Damian?'

'No, I think that's it, unless you've got anything?'

'Umm…, maybe one thing.' Damian was beer-emboldened and couldn't stop himself asking 'Is that the Phial of Galadriel you're wearing round your neck?' regretting his unseemly and over-personal question immediately, maybe he'd let himself down again, had he caused resentment? Offence?

'Damian, I'm surprised and a bit disappointed,' retorted Harry-Dan with surprising sternness. 'Surely you know better than to include this under "Any Other Business". It is not at all relevant to our meeting and cannot come under this agenda heading, let alone be referred to in the minutes. I'll tell you after the meeting. Is there anything else then?'

'No, I think that's it.' The needle on the dial was creeping back to the green zone.

'I love a well-timed meeting. Do you see the time?'

'5.30.'

'Whisky o'clock. Transgressive, no? No one expects it. A doubler?'

'No Butts Bank this time Harry-Dan? No hypocras?'

'Nothing to eat Damian, so there's nothing to close up. It's been beer all the way down.'

'Ok, thanks, yes then.' Harry-Dan whisked himself off to the bar where they'd both been umpteen times and was back just as Damian was about to get into a proper day-dream..

'There's one for the road. I brought some water in case you wanted it.' Damian always took water with his whisky being an inner-wheel whisky snob and H-D took some water as well.

'Beer all the way down!'
'Beer all the way down!'
Klink.
'Except for the Whisky!'
'Except for the whisky!'
Klink

'This...,' said Harry-Dan pointing to his pendant, 'this isn't what you said, the phial of Gladys or whoever. It is a "phial" though and contains a "philtre". Not this actual one, this is commemorative, it's like regalia if you like. This is what we can wear in public. I'm glad you asked me about it. Shall we go back on the beer?'

'What about halfs with whisky chasers?'

'Ideal.'

'I'll get them.'

15

A minute or two later and Harry-Dan was back with the beer
and filling in Damian about the philtre and the phial, divulging
all; it was a secret-society accoutrement which he wore in
a post-modern, knowing and ironic way. Most people didn't
recognise what it was and he was more than happy to put
Damian in the know on the inside track.

There were well-known ones, like the rosicrucians, knights
templar, freemasons, illuminati and what-not, and other ones,
like you get in America, like in the universities there, but
this was regalia of the most-secret, yet most-public society,
paradoxically in plain sight, but at the same time entirely
unknown to the hoi polloi and, ipso facto, the most successful
of them all. Harry-Dan seemed to be having a good time
letting the cat out of the bag and spared Damian no detail. If
true, it was incredible.

The philtre had been rescued from the burning library of
Alexandria and handed down through the ages by a mixed-
sex society who handed on the phial and the philtre through
the generations in a kind of historical association, the inner-
wheel of secret societies. Damian wanted to know what a
'philtre' was and H-D told him, but when Damian asked what
was so special about this particular philtre, Harry-Dan went
coy, returning to the story of the most secret and ancient of
historical societies, and saying its name out loud.

Damian heard the name as 'Autodidactiaye' but he'd missed
something both subtle and crucially important; Harry-Dan

had to try and spell it out for him out loud after Damian kept fumbling it.

'You've nearly got it. There's two "I"s before the "aye" at the end. Pay attention, I'll spell it out again for you:

A...U...T...O, auto,

D...I...D, did,

A...C...T, act,

I...I, aye-aye,

A...E..., spells "Aye". Have you got it now?' Confusion still reigned chez Damian.

'Look, it's not spelt like it sounds. The two "I"s are said Aye Aye, that's the letter "I", but put together they're said EE.. EE, not Aye Aye. The actual "Aye" in the word comes from A and E together, AE, which is pronounced "Aye". I'll say it again for you, auto, die, dact, EE-EE, aye. It's EE-EE AYE at the end. It's EE-EE AYE all the way down, do you get it?'

Damian had at last nearly got it, but it was a definitely a bit of a mouthful, he thought, and let Harry-Dan, looking a little frustrated, get back to his story.

'There was a bit of a hoo-ha just after the library burned down. Everyone was having hoo-has at that time and arguing about everything. Rancour abounded.' Damian was feeling slightly fobbed off with this nonsense, especially after the bizarre pronunciation thing, which had ended up being a bit embarrassing, why did people have to get their knickers in a twist about details all the time?

'A hoo-ha?'

'Hoo-ha, kerfuffle, yes. Anyway, there was a kind of dispute, got quite nasty at times, so they all got together for a council meeting to sort things out. Most of them wanted one mixed-sex brother-sisterhood but others wanted to break away and do their own thing. These dissenters called themselves "pedanti", "pedanticists", "pedanticians" or sometimes, all together, as an inclusive collective noun: "the pedantry" – in this country anyway. The society wanted all to be together as one, in love, peace and harmony, and so they found a formula, a touchstone, a shibboleth if you will; if a pedant could accept the name of the association then they would be welcomed to their respective chests and bosoms, and their pedantic ways as well. So, accordingly, built into the name was the deliberate "EE-EE AYE" bit, an obvious affront to pedantry. Think red rags. Think bulls. This was the only confession of faith they had to make and happily many did.'

'And what about the other ones?'

'Cast to the outer darkness. They wander the planet still with their tiresome, lonely and pedantic ways, picking fights, looking for brawls. Have you not heard the legend of "The flying Dutchman"? That's actually only an allegory. It's really about "The flying Pedant". They're not a threat as they start falling out with each other over trifles whenever they get together. They can't organise but they're out there.' Damian was secure in the knowledge that he wasn't a pedant. He was a big-picture person, although he didn't mind standing up for himself if someone got something wrong. 'There is always a home for them amongst the Autodidactiiae, should they so wish to so choose.' Harry-Dan paused again, his favoured rhetorical device. 'At least, that's the story.'

'Are you in it?'

'Damian, you jest! It's a story, made up, like Tolkein or Star Trek or that other one in space with the robots and magic kids. You don't think someone's a wizard if they buy a wand, do you? One more for the road?'

'Go on then.'

The transgressive afternoon session had moved into the promisingly dangerous early evening phase, but it was time for Harry-Dan to get back and they parted with Damian saying he would get right on it and Harry-Dan saying he would look forward to hearing from him and that Damian should keep him abreast of developments.

Damian flopped down on his bed-settee at home and went over it all in his head. He felt better about still not knowing what his enquiry should be about after the great session and the cathartic unburdening of his historical inhibitions. Somehow progress had been made. Should he perform some ritual to sanctify his new start? Make a gift of himself to the universe maybe? Too much, surely.

'C'est too much!' he said to himself. Damian's head was too full. He needed to digest, to compartmentalise. He was ready for it but how it would come to him? In the night like a beguiling succubus or would it need to be mastered and tamed like a wild mustang? He was getting tired so he put 'Glengarry Glen Ross' on the television to relax with the familiar and well-plotted film, which he never tired of watching.

The dialogue, the characterisation, the drama, the way it made you sympathise with these people. It was miraculous; how did they make up a story that you could enjoy over and over again, even when you knew the ending? These people in the film always did the same things and said the same things but there was always something else, something new to it, each time, and he watched it again with relish. This film wasn't chutney, it was top class, Premier Cru, unlike a lot of the rubbish out there and he would watch it with relish if he liked, over and over again. Thank you David Mamet, thank you big-name cast of top-class actors. It had been a pleasure again. Damian pootered around a bit, had some tweet and went to bed content.

He was up at the right time. Everything was right, he could tell. He made some coffee and went out to the place by the gate in the fields. There was something more than right this time, there was something else out there. He could feel it, like sensing a friendly ambush.

The first gulp of coffee and the first puff of his first cigarette and this was his first day and he looked to the part of the horizon where the sun was rising.

'What's the story? What is the story?' he murmured to the invisible host of birds who were filling the air with their songs. Bird song like a cheering crowd, cheering him on, willing him on, getting louder, wanting him to get there, to break through, to succeed. He was tuned into the music and could make out each singer's contribution, lift it out of the background and hear each one on its own, enjoying it for its own sake and then gently put it back into the massed choir.

'What's the story?' he asked the singers. Who'd written the score for this music? It was a masterpiece: a complete experience of sound, sight and smell. Wagnerian. He knew it was close. He gripped the top rail of the gate with his left hand, smouldering roll-up between the first two fingers and tasted some coffee. A little bird, a little robin, appeared on a nearby post and began to give the loudest chirp-whistle from such a tiny body – this must be the aria – it was so beautiful. He listened, loving it. The little bird stopped and looked at him, waiting. Damian now knew what to say. How to get the right answer. How to ask for it in the right way.

'What's the story... please?' and the answer came. It was obvious and had been right in front of him all the time.

'Thank you..., thank you..., thank you very much..., and good morning.'

16

Appearing eager to leave risked causing offence but the new idea was swirling in his mind like a dust-devil trying to metamorphosise and he wanted to get back home to get working. At the right time, having demonstrated his appreciation, and when the chorus itself seemed to be packing up, he got his things together, checked he'd left nothing behind and walked back to Epsilon Precinct.

A new dossier was needed or, more accurately, a sub-dossier to the Gaunt dossier, to be called 'Usurper', a strange-sounding word that needed looking up; 'to take possession without a legal claim', from Anglo-French 'usorper'.

Henry IV was the famous usurper of history and the story was that this wronged and goodly knight came back from exile to claim his rightful inheritance from bad king Richard II and ended up being king himself. All well-known, well documented and well told already, but maybe it was too well told.

Damian suspected there had to be more to it than that and began wading through his Gaunt research, turning over stones, looking underneath, searching, knowing that this time it was going to be useful. The EPQ was to be about that usurper and his usurping. But what was that tantalising niggle? He had come across something trivial before which was now important. What the blinking flip had it been? Rooting around in the gravelly pebbles, his fingers dislodged an embryonic memory which came to the surface in a bubble. Something about doomed Richard II and his food. Richard II: the popinjay prince, the comeuppance king, famous for bravely out-facing Wat Tyler when the Peasant's Revolt came to London and getting himself kicked off the throne – something about his eating habits.

Damian turned his digital treasure-chest upside down and emptied it out, staring at the screen, clicking, opening, scanning and closing. It had been a remark at the bottom of an internet page. Had he even copied it into Gaunt? Searching fruitlessly lay in the empire of doomak and he felt its presence in the room with him, maybe lolling in an arm-chair, a wry patronising smile on its thin lips, watching him comb through his notes.

'Woah! Woah! Woah!' There it was. 'Take that Doomak!' Not even a yellowed cutting in an overlooked digital scrapbook, labelled in a curiously unhelpful way, but more or less in the right place but lacking the reference, of course. Should he try and find it? A doomaky shiver was enough to prompt Damian towards the better decision. The pleasure of telling Harry-Dan that he was up and running was not to be resisted. Damian emailed: Subject: Gaunt, he would be post-modern and ironic. Also laconic. Message: Snark! That was perfect, better be sure. I repeat: Snark! Damian read it out.

'Chroniclers had said that Richard had starved himself to death and…', this was the hot potato, 'that, from what we know about his character, this would not be a surprise.' Hold hard and wait one. He rephrased it.

'From what we know of his character, it seems likely that he starved himself to death.' What is being said here? Damian punched through the citation and put himself in media res.

Two servants, trusted to keep the deposed king alive and well fed, were trying to come to terms with the discovery of his passing.

'Hey, it's Richard! It's Richard! He's dead!' said one, his voice all panic and alarm.

'That comes as no surprise to me. You know what he's like,' from another more rueful voice, a voice Damian would categorise as "the chatty one", 'Richard had, as we all knew, I told you before – remember? – the character of someone who would starve themselves to death and it was bound to happen sooner or later. I blame myself.'

'Do you blame yourself? Do you really? How hard did you try to nourish the poor sap?' butted in Damian but they couldn't hear him.

'I know we knew that, but I never really believed he'd do it. Now he's dead!'

'But no effort was spared.' rebutted the rueful chatty one. 'We had carte blanche to do whatever it took to get that obstinate self-starver to take some food, any food. It was fully resourced and funded but ultimately useless. In fact it was more than useless. It was counter-productive. And he was so devious, wasn't he? You could never tell if you were making progress with the dietary regime or he was trying to pull the wool over your eyes.'

'I was nothing to do with it,' said Damian, mistaking the notorious ambiguity of 'you' for a reference to himself, and feeling guilty by association.

'Not "you", I mean "one", anyone, anybody. Are you being deliberately obtuse or what? Butt out will you?' They'd ignored him before but now enough was enough so Damian had to promise not to interrupt again but went on to justify his intervention anyway.

'Guys, I'm not here to rock the boat. I am just a humble

seeker after Truth, that and no more. What do you mean "pulling the wool over your eyes"? Never mind, please go on. I won't butt in again. Tell me. Elucidate,' and Damian hoped he'd not caused any offence.

'None taken. We tried disguising his food in drinks but he got wise to that and demanded only water, only the purest water, in a special pitcher, would you believe?'

Ewer. It's ewer, not pitcher, thought Damian, the chatty one was being cavalier with the details; maybe he was hiding something? Damian pitched back in with:

'So he wasn't thirsting himself to death then?'

'Butt out big mouth, you said you wouldn't butt in again, anyway he drank water like a fish. Water wasn't a problem; the problem was the food. He started out slyly, but that was in his nature, as we found out. He would cover up what he didn't eat with, like, pie crusts, rinds or lettuce leaves, or drop it on the floor and say that he couldn't eat it because it was dirty. I used to say "It doesn't matter, it's just been kissed by the devil" because that's what my granny used to say to me, but it didn't help. He found all kinds of other ways as well.'

'What like?' interjected Damian and the chatty one, now habituated to Damian's interference, replied:

'Well, like we had to put a lock on the window as he'd be in the window seat reading a psalter or book of hours....'

'Yes, he had some of those funny pilgrim stories, you know, with rude bits in,' volunteered the alarmed one who had been quiet for a while. There was clearly some kind of a hierarchy thing going on between these two and the alarmed one wanted to show he wasn't to be ignored by sticking his oar in. 'Have you read any? My favourite's the one where ....'

'No, I haven't but yes, that's right, he read those all the time as well.' said the chatty one, put out by the interruption.

'He used to laugh out loud and snigger all by himself, do you remember?'

'Yes, anyway it would be a mealtime.' The chatty one was trying to keep it on track.

'Time for some tweet?' interjected Damian again, because it was irresistible.

'Yes, a mealtime, like I said, and I'd bring it to him and put it next to him on the window-seat and you'd look away...'

'You mean that "you" would. You and him, keep me out of it,' chided Damian, misusing his new-found familiarity with the fourteenth century turnkeys.

'Yes, ok, I or we would, or anybody who was there would, and the next minute he'd be licking his lips saying "yummy" with an empty plate in front of him.'

'How did that happen, perhaps he ate it?' Damian wanted to both drill down to the facts of the matter and be mischievous.

'No, he didn't eat it! It went out the window of course!' Methinks there petulance doth dwell, noted Damian, getting into it.

'We would find bits of it in the roses,' added the alarmist.

'Is that it?' Just that?' Damian wanted more detail.

'No there's a lot more. As I said, he was determined. He had a determined nature, but not in a good way, he was a bad king after all and got what was coming, otherwise he wouldn't have been there, would he?' Damian choosing not to rise to the bait, pushed further.

'Can you give me an example?'

'Easy. For example; he would sometimes say the food

was being served in the wrong order and that it had all got
mixed up in his stomach and it was drawing out his humours
and making him ill and he would eat it later when he felt
a bit better but then it would be too cold or too dusty or
whatever, there was always an excuse. A special chef was
brought over from France but, no, it was always too rich or
too creamy; why did you need complicated sauces, he'd say,
was it to cover up bad meat?'

'How long did this go on for?'

'It went on and on. We didn't really put two and two
together and when we did, he was already dead and it was
too late. I blame myself, well, myself and this other guy, who
should have known better and was, perhaps, also to blame.
Maybe even mostly. There'll have to be an enquiry.'

The alarmed one was rightly anxious at the way things were
going and tried to protect his position without appearing to
undermine the chatty one's authority too much; these were
medieval times, after all.

'Will that affect our Christmas bonus this year, do you
think?'

17

Richard had been imprisoned in Pontefract castle for up
to four months before his death on 14th February 1400.
Natural causes, suicide or murder, it had to be one or the
other. Or maybe it had been an accident; could it have been
manslaughter? How many smoking guns were there? And
something else was odd. Historians appeared to echo each
other's opinions and come to common conclusions. Agreeing
with each other. Incessantly quoting each other.

There was a universal slant and a shared tone; Henry IV was
the 'goodie' and Richard II was the 'baddie' and England was
better off without him. The same stock was being used to
make different soups. Had they tried soup with him? Damian
couldn't remember specifically but knew that the soup wasn't
the key in any case. What was key then? The key was in the
way the story of this man Richard was told. Told in the way
he didn't like, the history nonsense way, where each part of
the story was tailored to fit to another, to make the…, the…,
Damian wanted to have some fun and on a great day like
this, a triumphant breakthrough, who was there to deny him?
Nobody. He could ham it up to the max. To make the…,
the…, the abhorred word was forcing itself on him, fighting
with him, and this wasn't a play fight, it was getting nasty: each
bit of history was tailored and dovetailed together to make…,
(gag), to make…, (gag), to make a…, a…, a narrative! (gag,
retch, puke, spit) To make a lying deceitful narrative.

History had not been telling the truth and he'd cast

out its poison, like in those films where somebody has to take a bullet or arrow out of themselves with just a knife and gunpowder. Damian wiped his mouth with the back of his sleeve and went to the kitchen area for a cleansing drink of water to formalise his pretence before thinking it through. The verdict was unanimous; a bad king had died in a good cause and it was his own fault. His own internal contradictions had brought about his doom so let's move on. Damian was piqued and felt a mis-history of justice had been done. Historians had cobbled the story together like carpenters making a table or tailors making a suit of clothes and, as long as it all held together, as long as it made a reasonable jacket or reasonable piece of furniture that didn't wobble or split under the shoulders, it was a good bit of history. As long as the narrative was an accepted one, you could say what you liked. This story was very well embedded. One part of it was that the failed king may have colluded with his own death, so revealing a character-trait that was proof of his unworthiness in the first place. How else did History paint and narrate?

The country had been given the wrong king and a better man had come along; there had been some kind of mix-up and the right man had been deprived of his destiny by a changeling who should never have been there in the first place; a gallant and noble knight came to slay the dragon of despotism and restore the rights of the land, including his own. History had stepped in and sorted out the problem of Richard.

History, a river of progress winding towards the future, sinuously eroding out its anomalies on the inner bank of the bend and depositing better things on the outer one as it meandered along. Was Richard II like an ox-bow lake then? A cut-off, going nowhere. A pond. The writers agreed that he was, although sometimes there might be a little hint of 'Richard wasn't always as bad as all that' along with 'you know, sometimes Henry's motives were maybe not of the purest' surfaced, but in general you could say with certainty that they had one voice; the better man had come, so too bad: move over Richard, let Henry take over. Stand aside, you are toast, you are history!

Damian looked at Richard's last known address, Pontefract Castle, using Google Maps' satellite view and strolled around the town with Google Street View to get some fresh air, and fresh perspectives. There wasn't much to see of the castle as it had mostly been knocked down and blown up in the civil war but the whole lot had been pretty big. All mostly gone now, so you wouldn't be able to follow in Richard's footsteps or know where he spent his time.

Had Richard had the use of sumptuous apartments with roaring fires, great views and good company to while away the time playing backgammon and the lute, or did he spend his days crouching in a dark, cold and wet cell until he could conveniently expire? Where was Pontefract relative to the national network of roman roads? He whistled for his faithful Ordnance Survey Roman Britain 4th edition map that he knew was around somewhere and his old friend, heeding his call, came up him, tail wagging and looking for a tickle. The good old map was coming apart at the folds and couldn't really be handled without causing further damage, so he had to be careful with it. Surely it couldn't last for ever, a loyal companion, irreplaceable.

Pontefract was hard to make out on this map as modern detail wasn't what it was about, it was about things Roman, but he could just about see where Pontefract was, right on Dere Street which went from York to Edinburgh, right through Pontefract and on to Castleford, where a roman fort had been where it crossed the river Aire. The Aire looked to be quite a wide feature given the number of ponds and little lakes that dotted the area and it was definitely splodgy, especially back then. The Romans would have built a massive bridge there; they were known for that, but it was gone now. Pontefract was right by the M1 and he'd unknowingly bombed past it in his car many times over the years. He would look in one day.

The river Ure was crossed by the same road 50 miles to the North, next to the A1(M) motorway at Boroughbridge, another place he must have zoomed past blithely. Boroughbridge was hard to enunciate. Damian imagined his biscuit-filled mouth trying to say 'Borrow a fridge', you couldn't help but mumble it and he could only guess at what it sounded like pronounced in a local dialect where long familiarity had further smoothed its shy consonants. A battle had been fought there 75 years before Richard's death and Damian had an inkling there was a link.

A rebellious army had been escaping up Dere Street and loyalists wanted to stop them at the riverine pinch point. Damian had read Wang Chung's ancient treatise on how to win wars and river-crossing fights were classic instances. Basically you should let half your enemy cross a river and then attack. The royalist loyalists clearly hadn't read it because they didn't let anyone over unless they were dead, and that's how the Earl of Hereford got across, by being killed in a most unchivalrous manner. His co-rebel, Thomas of Lancaster, son of Edward I's brother was captured, taken to Pontefract and put to death there.

Wikkipedia ejected a curiosity like a lottery ball down a chute; within a year the victor was himself hung, drawn and quartered by Edward II for trying to make peace with Scotland. Tough times indeed. Damian mused and pondered. Was that when the age of chivalry could be said to be over? When they killed you instead of giving you a telling off? Not just killed, but killed cruelly and slowly in public like they used to do in the Coliseum? Edward I had started it off with William Wallace, but it had really taken off in Edward II's time.

More numbered and colourful balls came shooting out. Piers Gaveston, Edward II's right-hand man had been murdered by two Welsh varlets while the Earls of Warwick, Lancaster, Hereford and Arundel looked on, gloating and applauding. Lancaster and Hereford got their just deserts at Boroughbridge and it probably served them right but Arundel swapped sides, unfortunately to the losing one, and had his head chopped off later. Only Warwick walked away.

All these men's names cropped up two or three generations later and their reincarnations caused Richard II no end of trouble. Had the Gaveston murder been a kind of original sin which haunted history, looking for redemption, or had the unquiet ghosts of Edward II's reign been actively seeking to achieve with Richard II what they had failed to do before with Edward II; later characters being puppets animated by their implacable will. Had History been trying to do a proper job second time around? A better job?

Damian's break from work had taken an eerie turn and

he wanted another digression to relax. What about secret societies? He googled them and tried to copy and paste what it said about them into a document, but the text box stayed blank. It wouldn't copy. He'd tried five times but was baulked. It was sort of to be expected, although he'd been surprised, and he couldn't find anything at all about the Autodidactiiae. Not even a mention. That was unsurprising. It was the most secret one. He carefully pronounced the word and said it out loud.

'Auto, die, dact, ee-ee aye.' You couldn't look it up. No, you could look it up, but it wasn't there.

18

All of History was in accord; Richard had been a pain in the neck and everyone was better off without him. Damian's instinct pulled the other way but he didn't want to be a controversialist just for the sake of it, he wanted to be right as well, so he needed more. Thanks birdies, earthly agents of some otherworldly directing presence, they'd put him on the right track, so thanks and all that, but without wanting to be spiritually mean, why did they have to be so bloody Delphic about it, couldn't they have been more explicit? Oracles, portents and signs just gave hints, maybe hoping their ambiguity would trip you up and prove them right, but not the way you expected; that was the Delphic way.

Damian used the last of his internet energy to google about birds and learnt a lot about them in a short time. When he went on to investigate foreign birds, infrequent visitors to these shores, he knew he'd been over-doing it and needed a rest. He pushed the chair and laptop away, made himself a little nest and gave himself an afternoon lie down, stretching out on the couch, his head on a russet cushion.

This was the next best thing to active day-dreaming; a well-deserved nap, especially if it was that special time of day when everything was quiet and the intermittent passing of vehicles made a distant wooshing like the transgressive ticking of an irregular clock. That hushed time of day was to be cherished, it wasn't every day but you were having a nap and nobody outside knew. Transgressive. Dreamy. Ideal. The bloody little robin had been singing its bloody little song, no, its bloody big song, an aria. Was it singing to celebrate the joy of the morning, the little show-off, or was it more prosaic than that, a territory issue, or to find a mate? But the robin had stopped singing. It had stopped singing and looked back at him. It had looked right at him. Seen him.

A bright full moon shone through a triple-arched window of gothic tracery and funereal light lit the room with nocturnal tones of blue and silver. Laid out on a long trestle table, over which a white linen cloth had been draped almost to the floor, was a man's naked corpse. Its long, auburn hair lay about his shoulders and its head rested on a rolled-up cloth, the mouth and eyes closed, the limbs long, thin and wasted. Damian could see no wounds in the pale flesh but it was dirty and the fingers, hands and feet looked grimy. Had it been a drowning? Damian examined the face and took in every detail; the hair around the chin and mouth, the ears and mouth, the shape of the nose, the chin, the sunken cheeks and eyes, the life spirit had fled the flesh and left it sinking in on itself like a hollowed-out dead bird. There was someone else there.

A female figure stood at one side of the room, still, back to the wall, half in shadow; someone wearing a long, hooded dark-red cape, gathered at the front with a bright silver brooch which caught the moonlight, stood in the darkness with Damian, facing the corpse and holding a rosary. The realisation that what had brought him there was now drawing him away came the moment he saw her. Damian wanted to say something but couldn't break the spell of silence. He knew they'd been brought together for a reason but the moment was passing and he understood, with sadness, that the time had come for him to open his eyes.

Colourful and lurid dreams were as mother's milk to him but this one had stunned and he wanted to mark it somehow, maybe some overacting would do it, perhaps by dramatically reaching around as if blinded, flapping and floundering, puffing and blowing, maybe gasping, but he knew that forced theatricality was unworthy of what he'd been through. It would be truly bathetic and the vision deserved to be treated with more respect than that. He calmed himself down with a cup of tea and then tried to relive it. It wasn't hard to understand. It was about death and the dead man was Richard II. Damian hadn't seen a real dead body before and it had shocked him. Something needed to be said. Something that would permanently fix the scene in his memory.

'Oh the finality!' that worked well. 'Oh the finality! Oh the finality!' but repetition made it sound banal so he stopped and moved on.

What was that other person doing in the room with him? He resented her presence. Why would he be sharing his private vision with her? That woman. Who was she? Had she actually been sort of rude being there just standing around, enigmatically, in his private vision of the dead king. He would identify her and so rob her of some of her mysteriousness. Give her a code-name. He'd call her Romana Clay which befitted her toga-like robes and statuesque stillness. He checked 'Clay' for aptness and found plenty of quotations that could justify the word: biblical ones, mexican ones and one from Victor Hugo, so that's who'd she'd be, Romana Clay, and never 'The lady in red'. Over his dead body.

'Time to open a new sub-dossier,' he said, fragmentary monologues being a perk of his solitary life, and made a new one called 'Murder'. He wanted to spit on his hands and rub them together but was too eager and didn't have time to stop for that. It was mid-afternoon and he wanted to know all about Richard II and all the people around him and all the things that had happened. He trawled, scooped and netted assiduously, and it was heady, confusing stuff. There were only a few families involved and the same names kept coming up time and time again. They were all married into each other, like it was all basically the same family. All the similar names and titles made it hard to keep track of individuals. It was a confusing kaleidoscope of characters, stories and plots but Damian wouldn't stop or give in.

Hours later and darkness had fallen but Damian had cracked it. He had used Wikipedia, Excel, gone for gold and he had found his story. Henry IV was going down for this. Damian would make him infamous. It wasn't too late because the universe cried out justice. Damian was on the warpath but he needed some formality to mark the official start of his quest, to take some kind of vow. Could he knight himself? No, they would laugh at his presumption and mock him like a d'Artagnan.

He would go incognito to the temple and make a simple offering like the little drummer boy. In the temple he might be bidden enter the inner sanctum where the shaman priestess would offer him words of comfort. The unworthy would probably think her alluring but to him she was a professional shaman woman just doing her job. The statue of the goddess, on the other hand, in the courtyard on the way in, was very alluring indeed and he would have a good look at her on the way out, sneak a really good peak. He didn't want to act repressed, that would be unworthy, especially in a taking-of vows dream scenario. Behaviour worthy of a pedant. Not him.

Oaths and vows taken, Damian felt he needed to develop a more efficient information system. Something modern and progressive was needed; a new way of organising and accessing the data. A tactile index that you could write on, maybe made of card, that you could pick up, rearrange, shuffle around, add to, until it made sense, a bit like playing cards but with information on. He had a better idea. He would use envelopes.

They could be held in the hand like playing cards, you could lay them out and collect them into various categories, various piles and you could write a lot on them. Damian wondered if that was profound, an envelope with nothing on the inside and everything on the outside, and decided that, if it wasn't already, it would be by the time he'd finished.

He had another, even better, idea. He would use his calligraphy pen to write with and really enjoy the act of etching the words into the paper of the envelopes. He would hold fire on colour-coding for the moment though. Enthusiastic and excited, Damian sent Harry-Dan an email using a cliché which, although totally lacking in post-modern irony, was laconic. 'Eureka!'

Lorna would love this, he thought, and he went to work transferring important information to a large number of envelopes via a pen's steel nib, then came the colour coding. Damian was going analogue.

19

Damian had said goodbye to Dolmetscher half an hour ago and it hadn't gone well, so he was working a Cat Stevens tune into the rhythm of the journey and finding the two tempos a tight fit, almost discordant, the train's noise breaking into the melody not quite in the right place, while ruminating about the meeting.

> *My Lady D'Arbanville, lah, la-la-la...la-lah,*
> *diddly-dah..., diddly-dah...,*

Lorna was supposed to have been there to meet him but she'd cried off at the last moment and it was postponed. Damian hadn't got the message in time as he never carried his phone on him; it was normally left in his car for emergencies. She'd telephoned the office just as he'd arrived and they'd spoken on Dolmetscher's antiquated desk telephone, her voice sounding nasal and far away. He explained how he was doing, proudly sparing her no detail, and how he intended to deal with Henry IV, although he didn't mention the vision he'd had in case it came over as a bit airy-fairy. She had been all encouragement and warmth and the call ended cheerily when she said she'd heard her oven alarm going off which meant it was time to take her home-made fudge out. Damian could almost smell the hot buttery sweetness of it down the line.

But Harry-Dan's tone had changed and Damian, looking back, suspected that he'd been talking to Lorna about him before he'd got there. Where was the easy smile? Where was the bonhomie? Dolmetscher had been reserved, frosty. This meeting was a 'dry broach', a term unfamiliar to Damian, H-D said it came from engineering, and had as its object the arrangement of the final elements of Damian's EPQ prior to completion. It was to be regretted that Lorna had been obliged to drop out but that couldn't be helped and wasn't essential. There wouldn't be time for them to go to his later-lunchtime H.Q this time as H-D had other people to see and it was time to wrap things up and finalise.

Wanting to show how busy he'd been, Damian had brought out his 50 annotated envelopes with a flourish and made a show of putting them in little stacks on the desk, using them as props as he presented his new way of doing things, and they looked good, he thought, laid out in their various piles. He didn't get the enthusiastic reception he'd been expecting, almost the opposite. Harry-Dan had been…, had actually been…, had been critical. Time was running out. They were approaching the end of the cycle. There was a deadline. Yes, there could be extensions but there were two types of people in the world: those who needed extensions and those who didn't. If Damian wanted to properly complete the program with Lorna then more was needed, there was a schedule to keep to, and Damian was falling behind. There was even a real risk of rustication which meant going back to the first square in snakes and ladders.

It had all been downbeat and, after the butter-scotch high had worn off, kind of dreary. A downer. H-D had practically escorted Damian off the premises when it was ended. There had been no hypocrastic oaths, no chat, no fun this time.

Your lips look like winter, lah, la-la-la…la-lah,
diddly-dah…, diddly-dah…,

Damian stared through his reflection in the window to look at the passing countryside and was glad that nobody was sat in the seat opposite as once, much younger, he'd tried to 'stare out' the reflection of someone sitting there for about half an hour and had felt embarrassed about it ever since. It hadn't all been sour milk and stale buns. He'd had the chance to look at Harry-Dan's ink-stamps; there were twelve of them with an important-looking foreign one in the middle which said 'Erledigt'. Harry-Dan had almost brightened up when he'd remarked on it, saying that was the one he looked forward to using on the dossier he had on Damian, eventually. It was like the one ring to bind them all, the one stamp to stamp them all, and Damian wanted it so very much, but thought it impolite to ask where he could get one.

Had he read too much into Harry-Dan's demeanour? Damian didn't consider himself a gold medal empath, so maybe he'd taken things the wrong way. They had, after all, talked about the refurbishment of the R.A.F.A building which had been covered in scaffolding for repainting and the front door was different. The downstairs room was empty, the bar gone, old carpet and lino taken out and the pictures of fighters and bombers weren't there anymore, although they'd left brighter patches on the magnolia walls. The city council needed Harry-Dan's association to vacate the premises so they could be used as the city's Wellbeing-You! centre.

Demand for these services was soaring as people lost their inhibitions when it came to addressing their anxieties and hang-ups; dealing with wellbeing issues was becoming the new normal and more provision was needed so space for it had to be found. It was typical, H-D complained, that just when he'd got his desk the way he wanted, the final touch being the black vintage A3 notepad in pride of place so he could write telephone numbers down and doodle while on the phone, it was time to move on again, and he hoped his next place would be big enough to take his desk, but sometimes they didn't let you take your own furniture.

> *I'll wake you tomorrow, lah, la-la-la...la-lah,*
> *diddly-dah..., diddly-dah...,*

A group met weekly in a northern working man's club to help each other improve their accordion skills. Damian had joined them for a couple of months and he remembered earnest Stan, who'd been devoting his retirement to the instrument, along with gardening. A well-known comedy sketch has a bad pianist, on being rebuked by the conductor, stick up for himself:

'I am playing all the right notes, but not necessarily in the right order, sunshine.'

Stan played the right notes, in the right order but had no sense of rhythm whatsoever. It was astonishing. It was agonising. Everyone in the group of self-taught amateurs would listen attentively to him playing and at the end he'd get a ripple of polite appreciation and the next one would get ready to play their piece for that week. They were supportive and respectful, although Stan's playing was dreadful. Maybe everyone felt that they were all, in some way, like Stan. Earnest, hardworking but always a bit 'off' despite their best efforts.

But your heart seems so silent, lah, la-la-la…la-lah,
diddly-dah…, diddly-dah…,

Who was Romana Clay? Was she trying to worm herself into his thoughts disguised as Lady Darbanville? She'd already changed how he recalled his vision of the dead king. Damian knew he'd seen the king first, then her, but now he remembered them together, she standing by the wall and looking towards the recumbent body. That wasn't how it had been.

'Back off dollface!' is what he would say to her if it happened again, but she didn't have a face, it was hooded. She was the interloper here, not him. He'd been there first.

Perhaps better would be:

'Lady! Please, do you mind?' and kind of wave her away but he hadn't wanted to move, it might have been the wrong thing to do. Perhaps he could reimagine the scene and then, in a collaborative conspiratorial way, make a kind of 'pssst' sound and hope she would understand that he wanted to have a one-on-one, so could she please give him some space? He tried but he couldn't shift her out. There she stayed, impudently holding her ground against his 'psssts', pretending not to hear, looking at the dead king on the table in the blue silveryness of the night.

Get out Romana, lah, la-la-la…la-lah,
diddly-dah…, diddly-dah…,

That worked. That actually worked pretty well, it fitted the rhythm better. But you could go to places to look at dead kings. They had effigies on tombs in cathedrals. You could have a one-on-one with them there and she wouldn't be there. Richard II had a tomb probably. Other people would have. You could ask them questions, interview them, get their story. He could ditch his 50 envelopes. No, even better, he could keep them and stick internet pictures of tomb effigies on them and make them handy briefing fact-sheets for effigy interviews.

The revelation excited: he'd discovered an original perspective, he'd already found the important questions to ask, and he knew who he could approach to ask them. This needed formalising and he wouldn't go to the temple past the statue of the sexy goddess to see the comely priestess this time, instead he'd buy the bigger scooter in the better colour he'd seen online and get it accessorised to the max. The dry grasslands of his ambition had been set on fire by a bolt of inspirational lightning. Damian knew what had happened. He knew he'd been unblocked.

'I am unblocked,' he said aloud, exultant. Heads turned. He didn't care.

20

First on the list of people having first-hand experience of Henry IV's usurpation, and nearest to Epsilon Precinct, was Elisabeth of Lancaster, 1364-1426, currently residing at St Mary's Church, Burford, Worcestershire, which is why Damian had parked in a gravelled area outside some nice-looking houses by its churchyard, which he was nervously wandering around, getting his head together before going in to see her. He had a worry; was what he was about to do normal? Or was it weird? Weird like staring out someone's reflection in a train window, except this time he intended to talk to it. He'd seen people having imaginary conversations and he didn't want to come over like that. Maybe he could whisper, or would it happen noiselessly, on a higher plane?

'Structure it. Let's get the context clear first,' slipped innocently and unnoticed from his mouth. It was his first interview and he needed to prove that his methodology would bear scrutiny. He needed to maintain an appropriate objectivity and not ramble on. Nor fall for any flim-flam from them. Damian found a convenient wooden seat to sit on and pulled out a wad of envelopes. Fifty had been reduced to twenty-five as not every personage involved in the affair had a tomb. There was discipline built-in, there were rules he'd stick to and he liked that, he wasn't going to make it easy for himself.

Most people in this situation, he thought, having poured themselves a cup of tea from the small flask carried in their knapsacks, would now get out their handheld devices and start doing things on them, but to him these devices were suspect and contained a lurking doomak potential, so he didn't have one. He was here and in the moment now. Where he was, was where it was at.

He fanned out the envelopes in his hand, rearranged a couple and pulled out Elizabeth's. Who was she? Second child and second daughter of 'Big' John of Gaunt and 'Bodacious' Blanche of Lancaster. Big John had got himself all the Lancaster family loot by marrying her and she'd been, by all accounts, booty-full in every sense. Only three of their seven children had survived and Elizabeth was the middle one, three years older than the future Henry IV. Her elder sister Phillipa had an attractive tomb in Portugal and Damian hoped to have an excuse to visit it one day.

She was lying on a tomb-chest, lying on it was called 'gisant', a special word for when you had an effigy on a stone box and you wanted to say it was lying on top. She was unusual as she was painted in muted but bold colours, and lay modestly but grandly dressed, hands pressed together in prayer, a circlet or corona – basically a posh Alice band – on her head over her shoulder-length blond hair. Her face had obviously been taken from life; it was long and full with a little prominent chin, a strong nose, lines between her mouth and cheeks which hinted at her age, 61, thin rouged lips and sticky-out ears, her head resting on a green cushion supported by little figures of monks.

Damian's internet exertions looking for effigies had fostered a respect for their artistic worth as sculptures but they were often ignored as works of art. Was it because they were gisant and not standing up? He marvelled at the great skill needed to fix these people in stone for eternity. Maestro stonemasons could find themselves a nice little sideline in effigies when they weren't building castles and cathedrals, carpenters as well as many had been made of wood, for the lower ranks, mostly all gone now. Alabaster was the favoured material. Almost marble but much easier to work with and available in England. John of Gaunt had been one of the first to use it. He would. He was used to the good things of life.

One of the important things about these effigies was their accuracy. Their fleshly counterparts needed their representations to be as life-like as possible. If not, something might go wrong on judgement day. They'd wanted to show themselves to God as they saw themselves in life, meek and pious or dressed up to the nines in the very latest fashions to show their earthly status to best effect, gisant, open eyes staring upwards, looking for the resurrection, however long that took.

A comical thought-reflux made him spasm, snort out his nose and accidentally take in some tea up the wrong way. He hadn't done himself too much damage but he smiled and chortled as he realised that what he really wanted to do right now was to put off seeing Elizabeth, defer the gratification and wander off for a bit or, even more decisively, to leave and come back another day. He laughed at himself, sniggering with self-awareness. The benefits were understandable. It was an attractive option. Was the determined decision to definitely do something another time really procrastination? Wasn't it the self-assured and fully-rounded personality that was able to show a situation who was the boss by putting it off? He would have enjoyed doing that but there were other visits to do, so he'd better get on with it.

How should he address her? Being beyond worldly cares he didn't expect her to be too sensitive to courtesy titles and would just call her by her name but he wouldn't do what he normally did in a church and loiter around shuffling between inscriptions and statuary and get to her almost by accident, sort of creeping up on her. He would be confident and go directly up to her using a stride adapted to the ecclesiastical mood. But it wouldn't be a slow march. That might be misunderstood as sarcasm. He didn't want to strike any wrong notes, draw any attention to the difference in status between them, she being dead and he alive. It would be more like a hospital visit. He could stand at the foot of her bed and pretend that things were normal, see how it went.

Damian gobbled down a corned-beef and mustard sandwich and washed it down with tea. Then he packed up, had a look around and walked into the church to see her.

21

'What's the story please?' he whispered after getting in position. The silence surprised. Uncomfortable seconds ticked by. He adapted his first-contact protocol.

'What's your story please?' There was the quietest little sob, followed by a sniff. A double sob, another sniff, and a last unclenching sob heralding a gathering air-raid siren wail of suppressed primal pain which gained steady momentum until the critical point was reached and out blasted a paroxysmic scream of anguish rent with sub-wails, hacks, and hiccups, making Damian uncomfortable and tense. He had woken the dead and the material he was getting was going to be unusable. Typical! She was upset but was it his fault? Had he caused offence? Had he upset her. He wanted to comfort her, but actually preferred to leave, but couldn't, not with her in that state. Matters might be made worse in some unpredictable way, so he'd have to see it through.

Damian retreated into a tonicly immobile safety-zone and soon enough the emotional outburst began to subside and crying, sobbing and hiccuping began to displace the wailing until at last it tailed off into sniffs and gulps for breath. Then silence and a last small sniff.

'I blame myself. I blame myself. I blame myself, I really do. I blame myself.' A pause. Then, with the certainty of the flagellant on their first day, came an authoritative 'I am to blame.'

He wasn't a qualified psychologist but even he could tell that this person wanted either to come clean about the terrible crime they'd committed or were wrapped in self-loathing, having got caught up in something that went horribly wrong, not their fault as such, although they clearly felt responsibility for the awful outcome. Either way, they needed some therapy.

'Elizabeth, maybe I can help you? Do you want to talk to me about it? Do you want to tell me what happened?'

'Thank you. Thank you. I do. I do so very much want to.' Television had trained Damian in the rudiments of how counsellors worked out client's neuroses and Elizabeth was already gisant so now was the time to go in with the right question.

'Why do you blame yourself then?' There was some sniffing. Had he gone in too hard?

'Thank you for coming. Thank you for coming. It's been such a very long time. I think I'm ready. I want to tell it, to tell it to you. Give me a moment please,' and some minutes passed. Damian made himself passive and patient until he was about to interrupt when Elizabeth happily obliged just in time.

'I sense you know much, but you don't know all. I'm to blame because..., because..., I started it all. It was all my fault.' Damian would have liked to butt in and ask 'all what?' but thought better of it and hung back.

'All we children loved playing together. We loved dressing up all the time but it was especially fun at Christmas. Everyone could be a bit silly, even the adults, even if they weren't normally. Phillipa and I always liked pretending to be princesses and we had some clothes in a special box mummy made for us. We got to put on a special show for the adults on the Feast of the Epiphany, 6th January, Three Kings day, it was me and Phillipa acting out stories about princesses. Then Henry came along and there was a little toddler for us to play with and we loved tickling him and making him do things. He was our little prince to play princesses and princes with.'

It all sounded fine to Damian so far, quite jolly.

'Yes it was fine at first, and jolly, playing at princesses and princes at Christmas. It was fun.' A long pause. 'But ..., but ..., then one year our daddy really did become sort of King of Castile in Spain when Henry was turning 4 and I was 7 and Phillipa and I made a big fuss of being real princesses, and of our real little princeling, little Henry.

"Our Daddy's a real king now so Phillipa and I are real princesses and dear little Henry, you are a real dear little prince and we can all live in a big magic castle together", is what we used to say when we were dressing up. We had special robes and crowns as well. "Henry, one day you can be king and we can be queens, beautiful queens."

That make-believe dressing-up went on for a couple of years until we got too old and then Henry went away to learn how to be a knight and it was over. You know the rest.' Damian did know the rest but wanted it to come from Elizabeth; it would be more direct, more powerful, more convincing. Damian needed Elizabeth to go on but she seemed to have got it off her chest and was silent. He needed to prod her, provoke her. What would the therapist on a TV show have said?

'Could you tell me a bit more?'

'You are cruel!'

'It's for the best,' said Damian, therapeutically.

'Alright. Our father, John of Gaunt, set himself up as King of

Castile in the Savoy palace in 1371 and he acted as a king until they paid him a fortune to forget about it when Constance, Henry's sister by a different mother, married Prince Pedro in 1388. Constance became queen of Castile in 1390 and Phillipa became Queen of Portugal in 1387.'

'You shouldn't blame yourself. It all turned out ok, Henry did get to be king after all.' Here Damian was being cruel.

'Excuse me, what are you talking about?'

'Well, it all turned out okay in the end, didn't it? He became king Henry IV.' There was silence. Then in carefully measured tones, betokening suppressed rage came:

'It turned out okay at the end, are you effing joking, pardon my jeffing French you effing jeffing idiot mortal. It didn't turn out okay at the end. It was a total bloody catastrophe and brought us to ruin. That's what I'm to blame for, you stupid, idiot, mortal-man.' Damian said nothing, too taken aback.

22

'Did you think I was to blame for giving him too many sugary comfits at Christmas? For spoiling him with glacé cherries and combing his hair too much? But it sort of makes a stupid rotten sense that I should have waited all this time to tell my stupid story to stupid you, you stupid lummox. Let me spell it out for you. I am to blame for making Henry do what he did. I made him a king when he was a toddler. Phillipa and I crowned him over and over again and this is what he did to us when he took it from Richard:

One. My darling husband John was murdered in the most horrible way by that Arundel countess witch, one of Henry's gang. John was trying to get away and she got him and put him in her castle and then invited her family to come over and watch him being killed. All his friends were killed as well because that slimy cousin of Henry's, Edward of Norwich, had got them all to talk about maybe getting rid of Henry because he'd only been on the throne a couple of months and loads hated him and of course he got a lot of takers. Then he and his dad Edmund of Langley, another slimeball, tell Henry about it. That's the story. Very convenient don't you think? Henry has a great reason to kill them.

They said that John and some others were going to go to a party, on the 6th January, the Epiphany, dressed as pantomime characters, and kill Henry. Can you believe that? My John, renowned John Holland, chivalry's first knight, dressing up as a morris dancer to assassinate the king? An effing morris dancer? Kill Henry at a Christmas pantomime, get away with it and live happily ever after? The only part of the so-called 'Epiphany Rising' that was true was the epiphany that Henry had when he decided that now was the time to deal with the loose ends. 'Epiphany Terror' more like. He killed them all.' Elizabeth was calming down, becoming more discursive.

'I so loved John, we were like a glamorous famous couple. He was a perfect knight, and hot, that's for sure. Hot-headed and hot in other ways. We were so alike.' Was she getting wistful?

'Thanks Elizabeth, what else can you tell me?'

'Just let me carry on, will you? Don't interrupt.

Two. Have you any idea how many of my family were killed because of Henry? John's brother Thomas, for one. Not strictly my family, I know, but John wouldn't have liked me not to mention him. From my family there was aunt Joan's grandson exiled and his son executed, Aunt Mary had 2 sons executed and a grandson as well, and Aunt Eleanor's grandson was killed.

Three. What was all the killing for? Who needed Henry? We were set up for peace with France. It was my father's plan and all the pieces were in place; it's what people wanted. Henry wanted war to give his soldiers some action but parliament had him by "les couilles", you call them goolies, and wouldn't give him enough money so they'd have to let their war wait until Henry V to get it going and he didn't have much choice did he? Have a good war or you're just the son of a bloody usurper, poor Henry; what choice did he have? And what was the result of those stupid wars with France? The stupid wars which everyone knew we couldn't win in the end, that we'd never been able to win.

We should have defended what we had. Aquitaine and
Gascony were lovely. We could have protected them. That
was always daddy's plan. We needed to protect what we had
already, not gamble on a big win. King of France? Ridiculous!
Countless were killed and we lost it all in the end, then they
all fought each other in the Wars of the Roses – killing and
killing and killing until there was no blood left.' Elizabeth took
a short break and came back.

'You know I lost a son in a French war?' Damian did know.
'He was killed standing next to his father. His head was shot
off by a cannonball. That changed him.'

'I bet it did,' quipped Damian helplessly, ungallantly,
soundlessly and happily unheard.

'He only wanted to kill non-Christians after that; he was a
better man from then on. But that wasn't my first John, John
Holland, that was the John I had to marry next. John who
brought me here. He was alright, loved my father, but a bit of
a bumpkin. Came from Cornwall, that was his name as well,
can you imagine? My first John was killed in 1400 and they
made me marry the other John the same year. You'd think I
would have minded but actually he and the other Cornwalls
in the neighbourhood wanted to protect me and marriage
was the best way, otherwise some other slimeball of Henry's
would have got me. It's nice enough around here but a bit dull
and he wasn't often at home. But it was safe enough…, and
not too bad…, some nice people next door….' Elizabeth was
beginning to ramble, obviously getting tired, but Damian hadn't
quite got what he'd come for.

'So why were you to blame?' Was that the sound of his own
heart beating, pounding in the treacly silence? He wanted a

killer sound-bite nailing Henry as a narcissistic psychopath but Elizabeth wouldn't play ball.

'Who else are you going to see?' Damian went through his list of interlocutors.

'Say "hello" from me…, she suffered a lot, be more gentle, could you? …, that's not actually him you know…, rotten scoundrel, tell him to go to hell!'

Her voice was getting weak and she seemed to be fading quickly so Damian went into cheerio mode.

'Thanks. Thanks a lot for everything. It's been really useful. Can I come back if I need some details filling in?'

'Of course you can. Thank you for coming, come any time. Thanks for listening, I feel a bit better. Can I give you a tip?' Damian felt a breakthrough coming and chanced some informality,

'Thank you Elizabeth, please do.'

'Don't eat cucumber skin, its indigestible. It does the opposite of what you eat cucumbers for. They're supposed to open you up, and they do, but not with their skins on.' Damian was reminded of when his own granny had asked him to promise not to sit on cold walls. Elizabeth seemed to have found peace after all. Was that 'closure'? Her depth of feeling had intimidated but hadn't she just been forgiving of him, witness her concern for his digestive welfare despite his clumsy questioning? Not so for Henry IV, that was certain.

'I promise.'

'Thank you. Goodbye.'

'Goodbye to you.'

23

Spots of rain were smudging the dry ground as he got back into his car in a hurry to make some notes. It had been sunny and warm but the sky had suddenly darkened and an unexpected downpour washed the wind-screen with its tears. Damian enjoyed the temptation to pathetic fallacy. Elizabeth had been kind and useful, if a bit prickly, and she'd given him the best of all possible starts, real insight into what he was looking for. He checked through the important points.

Point A: had Henry been conditioned from an early age to think of himself as a king even though he was far from the succession? You couldn't say for sure that his sisters had put a little golden crown on his little head but the rest about their father, John of Gaunt, as king of Castile and Phillipa and Constance becoming queens, was fact. It could quite possibly have been as she described. It wouldn't be stretching it too far. Was there a hint of a personality disorder in Henry? A Napoleon syndrome? It was known to develop in childhood, and there was evidence of a lack of empathy in the way he liquidated his enemies. No trial. No mercy.

Point B: Elizabeth had said that the Epiphany Rising was more a cover story for an organised terror. This type of ruthlessness, somebody protecting their gains by liquidating their enemies, happened regularly in history: banging on doors at night, shouts of 'Treachery! Treachery!', round-ups, disappearances. This 'Rising' had been spectacularly unsuccessful and all its leaders, and many others, were killed.

No question of a trial for any of them. Successful for Henry though.

Point C: Elizabeth saw Henry's actions and legacy as being entirely violent and 'un-kingly', so where was his legitimacy? What had Henry done that was an improvement on Richard? Wasn't the story that of a 'bad' king being replaced by a 'good' one? Elizabeth hadn't anything nice to say about him, but maybe that was to be expected.

The enquiry had clarified and he didn't need all the tomb-people envelopes so he softened the blow by conjuring up his favourite lone-piper-playing-a lament soundtrack as he discarded as many as he could.

Elizabeth had wanted him to say 'hello' to Maud Frances but she would have to go. Maud's husband was murdered at Cirencester in the same rising that did for John Holland. Damian didn't need any more colour. He wanted meat not sauce and hoped that Elizabeth would be none the wiser. Who else?

Sir John Beauchamp and his wife in Worcester cathedral. The tomb had his name on but there were doubts. Damian wanted a first-hand account of the well-named Merciless Parliament of 1388 in which Sir John and others had been fatally victimised. Damian knew this wasn't Sir John but some other local bigwig. Executed traitors didn't get massive tombs in cathedrals unless they were archbishops. Out he went, inconveniently.

Richard Neville, 1st Earl of Westmorland lying between his two wives in St Mary's Church, Staindrop, County Durham? Great effigies the three of them, but out. Not the main man.

Margaret Holland between her two husbands in Salisbury

cathedral? He would have wanted to talk to the big-nosed one on the left, hard-nosed John Beaufort, but again, not key.

Thomas de Beauchamp 12th Earl of Warwick was represented by his wife's brass in St Mary's Warwick. He was important but history thought little of him and even Wikkipedia had little to say. If that had been his plan, to inhabit the shadows, then it had worked well. Too shadowy.

Henry V was in Westminster Abbey and Damian had been looking forward to a good chortle; he would have been able to say to him:

'Henry, you're looking good' and get the reply:

'Thanks, they gave me a new head in 1971.' A potential double chortle as his wife Catherine de Valois was there as well, basically just a wooden head, and he could have said:

'You're looking good doll-face,' to her, and she actually had a doll's face. But again, sideshows.

Thomas of Woodstock's wife Eleanor de Bohun had a brass on a plinth in Westminster Abbey. It would be for another time.

What about Edward III? And queen of his heart, Phillipa of Hainault? Groovy hair-do Pippa, dig the Gandalf look Eddie. No.

The Black Prince in Canterbury? No thank you. He was obviously a homicidal maniac, check out those gauntlet knuckledusters. He looks like he knows how to use them, likes using them, likes smashing people's faces in with them. Probably his favourite weapon.

Four big name witnesses left, and four others, for local colour. All the maybes were out, leaving the definitive eight: four central and four colourful. That was the job done.

Damian sat making plans until he'd sorted it all out and drove to fill up at a petrol station where he bought some tweet and some wine. His heart was singing. He'd get back, pull up the drawbridge, watch a film, wait for tomorrow.

24

The twin towers of York Minster looked down with indifference on Damian leaning against their consecrated stones, people-watching. It wasn't an activity that held any great attraction to him per se but he had nothing else to do right then except spy on strangers and think about what he had come there for. Passers-by were walking around chugging from spouted coffee cups which dredged up a comforting memory of using a plastic mug with a spout-lid for orange squash when he was an infant. It looked odd, walking around with a cup in your hand and sucking from it like that, looking like you were running late for something and should have a bacon roll in the other hand, the hand you were holding your smartphone in.

Damian disagreed with it. Why couldn't they take it easy, sit down for a minute and take things in. He couldn't condemn too much; he was a laissez-faire moralist when it came to new social norms, however annoying they were.

Face coverings were hardly anywhere now. Not here anyway. You'd had to get behind it at the time, conform to the new norms, but there'd been alienation all the same. That first covid summer, how many spooky be-masked, be-hatted people wearing dark glasses had he seen? Weird but it couldn't be helped. Discomforting. Distressing. Occasional vape clouds reminded him of fumigations. It was mostly all over, and about time, just the anxiety fall-out to clear up.

A woman wearing a tee-shirt splashed with the Wellbeing-You! logo crossed his field of vision. Well done you. You wear it well, pretty lady, you wear it very well indeed and well done Rick and the Spirogyra agency, things were definitely taking off for them. She was wearing ballet shoes and he tried empathising with her but feeling the smallest variation in the pavement and every tiny stone and piece of grit through his feet started to make him grumpy and uptight. He felt sorry for her; how she could get through her day without being negatively affected by her chosen footwear? What was the name of the mood he was in? It was a good mood and he decided it must be 'ebullient', from 'bouillir', to boil. He was boiling over with good soomaky vibes.

A cool-looking young dude with all the trimmings came into view and stopped by a bin to rest his coffee cup and check his device. His T-shirt had 'Anxietyup-Yours!' on. Damian debated the ethics. Challenging? Offensive? To some, certainly but Damian didn't want to live in a repressed world. There had been too many people being officious and telling people what to do. Some people had seemed to relish it. New trends didn't take long to pop up so well done Rick for getting Wellbeing-You! out there and shaping the narrative. Damian gave his erstwhile colleague a nod of approval and imaginated his own rip-off slogan: 'Live and let live' on the front with 'or get stuffed!' on the back. What would the woman with the ballet shoes look like in that?

Damian had been home after seeing Elizabeth in Burford, had emailed Harry-Dan Dolmetscher with an enthusiastic report and received a big screen-filling smiley face back from him almost immediately. He'd tweeted, boozed, watched something and then turned in early, ready to carpe diem the hell out of the next day, which was today, and got to Lincoln Cathedral to see Katherine Swynford in well under three hours after leaving Epsilon Precinct.

She had been John of Gaunt's long-term lover and, for his last three years, wife, giving him three sons and a daughter out of wedlock, i.e. from their liaison prior to matrimony, and had been by his side, or closer, for thirty years. She knew him well, that was for sure. Damian wanted to know more about the relationship between the great man and his son, Henry IV, and hadn't been disappointed. Katherine didn't have an effigy, just a big stone chest tomb and she'd been expecting him. Talking about John of Gaunt was her favourite subject and on and on she'd gone, needing no encouragement.

Henry was Big John's only son and heir. They'd done a few chivalric French ride-outs together to parlay and had also forayed into Scotland to fly the flag when Henry was 17. Nothing too dangerous. But a little later, in 1386, Henry aged 19, Big John left him behind to go it alone. Well, alone with everybody else, except Henry. Henry was left behind in Plymouth when he sailed off, with his entire entourage, his entire retinue, including Henry's sisters, to Spain, leaving Henry on the quayside, waving his hanky to those on board. They waved back, as the ships sailed away and didn't return until 1389, to deal with the emergency caused by Henry and his cronies.

The idea of Henry with the hanky could not be called a historical fact but Damian knew it was as true as any other conjecture he'd come across in the stories they told in history. It couldn't be proved but was true anyway. Well, you couldn't actually be sure he'd waved but Henry had definitely been there and they had sailed off. Maybe he had kept his hands in his pockets and whistled or maybe turned his back on the departing ships, pretending to have seen a friend approaching from a distance and waved the wrong way. Or maybe just with his hand and no hanky. Perhaps he'd overslept and missed them. Of course he'd waved them off with his hanky but why did Big John leave him behind? Only son, maybe he wanted to minimise the risks? But he had taken everyone else. The cat was away and it was time for a house party.

By the time Big John and the lot of them came back three years later Henry had become a big problem and caused a lot of trouble which had needed a lot of sorting out, schmoozing and paying people off. Big John of Gaunt still loved his prodigal son but it was a different kind of love, more a long-suffering official love. Katherine disliked Henry for all kinds of reasons and she had been more than willing to elaborate on them, but the main thing for her was that Henry, when he got to the throne, barred Big John and Katherine's sons, his own half-brothers and sisters, from the succession, which she thought mean. But they'd also done well out of Henry too, she admitted, and his step-family had given Henry some tough step-brothers for him to lean on, albeit they were effectively, but not actually, eunuchs. Henry wanted it all for himself. There could be only one one and only.

Damian had got rich pickings from Katherine, thank you kindly ma'am, so he turned his horse's head northwards, spurred its flanks with the heel of his boots and rode off up the A15 towards York, which is where he was, leaning against the indifferent Minster with a coffee in his hand, smoking and people-watching, not rushing, ebullient and taking it easy.

25

York, Eboracum, Jorvik, Everwyk, York; from the celtic for 'place of the yew', Évry and Ivry in France had the same origin. Two proper roman emperors had died there and the son of one of them was declared Emperor in York by his soldiers, going on to build Constantinople and christianity. Damian would have liked to see the world war two bomber-pilot's names in Betty's Tea Room but put it off so he could focus on with what he was there for, which was to see Archbishop Scrope. It was an odd-sounding name but who was he, Damian Email, to judge.

Not many Archbishops had been murdered in England and Scrope was the other, less famous, one. This Archbishop of York had been through the whole of Henry's thing and Damian was here to get the Archbishop's take. The Scrope envelope gave useful details: just a tomb-chest, no effigy, he'd been a cleric under sly Thomas Arundel, Bishop of Ely, a major player, and risen quickly under him to become Bishop of Coventry and Lichfield in 1387. Scrope's patron, Thomas Arundel, what a career he'd had: Lord Chancellor 1386-1389, Archbishop of York 1388, Archbishop of Canterbury 1396. Archbishop Arundel really was a bigwig. Archbishop of York is a bigwig but not as big a bigwig as the Archbishop of Canterbury. These two were a pair, one had groomed the other for high office.

What was he going to say to this Scrope who'd been right there at the very moment when Richard II was deposed and was one of the three spiritual lords: Archbishop Scrope, Archbishop Arundel and Bishop Trevenant, who announced Richard's deposition to parliament and then actually accompanied Henry IV to the vacant throne, sat him on it, and made him king of England on the 30th September 1399. You couldn't get any closer to the action. But it hadn't worked out for him. He'd got a rebellion going in the North in 1405 which, going the usual way of rebellions, went wrong; Henry Percy, 1st Earl of Northumberland fled to Scotland and Archbishop Scrope, Thomas Mowbray and Sir William Plumpton were executed. Did he need to know why the Archbishop had changed sides? There was a high risk of conjecturising here. Probably best to stick to what was definitely known. Play it by ear. Damian got up to get on with it. It was another chest-type box tomb. No effigy. Damian was beginning to miss the human contact.

'Archbishop Scrope.'

'Yes.'

'Would you like to tell me your story, please?'

'Yes.'

'Please.'

'Thank you. I know you know much and I'm not proud of some it. Which part can I help you with?'

'Well Archbishop, I sort of want to leave that to you. What is the most important part of it to you, would you say?' Damian was trying to take a sensitive tack. The archbishop had been part of the regime and then fallen foul of it. How would he exculpate himself?

'I know what it is…,' a long pause. 'I died in Christ in an execution personally supervised by Henry himself and Thomas

Mowbray was killed beside me. The Chief Justice of England was there and wanted us to have a proper trial but that's not how Henry wanted it to go down. Henry said 'get it done' and his step-brother, along with Arundel's whelp of a nephew made it happen. They did it not far from here.' Painful memories were coming back to the Archbishop but it wasn't the pain of being killed, something else was rankling him.

'Go on.'

'But that's not what I want you to understand even though it's a squalid thing surely, for a king to just decide to kill an Archbishop, without a trial, just like that, don't you think?'

'Yes Archbishop. Squalid and illegal too.'

'Yes. No, it's before that happened. It's the battle.' Damian knew about this. The battle of Shipton Moor was all over the back of his envelope; there'd been no fighting and history said that nobody had died. Two armies had met up and there'd been a stand-off for two days. 'Neville led their army. I liked him. We were all intermarried up there. Scropes, Nevilles, Percys. Henry's son John was nominally in command, Neville under him, until Henry got there later. We got to talking, us and them, in a parlay. These kind of things were well understood and had been done for hundreds of years. Chivalry you know. There were lots of formalities; heralds would go to and fro with messages and expressions of good faith, tokens would be exchanged.'

'Tokens?'

'Yes, we had our liveries, badges and emblems that we would exchange with the other party to show good faith.'

'Were oaths taken, sworn, or otherwise made?'

'They were taken, sworn and made, yes. Promises too, with

undertakings and agreements. It took two days and finally it was all properly concluded, according to the traditions and conventions of the age, in the sight of God.'

'Then what happened?'

'We disbanded our army and sent them home.'

Damian wanted to say 'And then what happened?' again, but decided against it as he already knew.

'Then they grabbed us, tied us up and took us as prisoners to Pontefract.' The archbishop went on to explain that what disgruntled him most was this betrayal, this breaking of pledges, this deceitfulness, this godlessness. Much had been taken, sworn and made but nothing was kept. It had all been broken.

'That was the day chivalry in England died and that's what I want you to know. What I want to tell you. There had been ups and downs before and it had been getting rocky, but there, on Shipton Moor, what they said meant nothing. Nothing. They were men of no faith. No honour. We were right to rebel against them. I have no regrets. Their faithlessness proved us right. We were worthy of our deaths but not in the way they thought. We were worthy because we were the better men. We were Christians. We were Christian knights with a code, with honour, and we died with honour. They had no honour. We died in glory, martyrs. He was not worthy to be a king. He was not worthy to be king. He was not worthy of it. Thank you for hearing me, young man.'

There was another one who'd wanted to get something off their chest.

'Thank you Archbishop,' and Damian gave his most thoughtful and grateful nod, almost reverential. 'Thank you very much.'

'One more thing before you go.'

'Yes Archbishop?'

'It's scroop.'

'I'm sorry.'

'No, my name, it's pronounced scroop.'

'Thank you Archbishop, sorry about that.'

'Not your fault, they all make that mistake, goodbye then.'

'Goodbye.'

Damian spent no time getting back to his car, pausing only to glance through Bettys' window to think of the bomber boys but couldn't see their names on the mirrors, and hit the high road South. He'd done well and planned to treat himself with a digression, hardly even out of his way, to the Isle of Axholme.

There was an elusive character in the story who didn't have a tomb. Thomas de Mowbray, 1st Duke of Norfolk, had been in Henry's gang in the early days but ended up exiled and died in Venice on the way back from a pilgrimage and it was his son, 20-year old Thomas junior, who'd been executed with Archbishop Scrope in Pontefract. Mowbray senior was almost exactly the same age as Henry. They had been partners in an earlier coup d'état against Richard II yet Henry, before he was king, picked a fight with him and they both ended up exiled.

Damian had found a reference on the internet, which he'd since mislaid, saying that the Isle of Axholme was the Mowbray's spiritual home and that their bones might have been returned there. That couldn't be proved and some Mowbray bones had been put in St Katherine's Chapel, near the Tower of London. Later in the day he was there, eating a sandwich he'd bought, washing it down with what was left in his flask He'd done very well indeed, he smugged to himself, with two most interesting testaments in the bag, and now it was time to enjoy a leisurely follow-through. Flicking his cup clean, he packed up his stuff and went for an amble around. The village of Haxey graced the top of what had been a little island in the Lincolnshire wetlands and it gave good views all around. What had been plashy marshes were now green fields and Damian thought about the weight of geological time needed to make this small sandy hill stand out like this.

Far off, he saw the multiple cooling towers of a power station. 'Yes, we all need electricity but it was a bit of an eyesore all the same,' was the ambivalent theoretical reconciliation he used to justify a sage but self-conscious nod of his head before packing his things away ahead of a saunter around the plain little church. He mooched all around it and then left the churchyard by a little gate to come out into the village next to a touristy information board thing, which he read, provoking a hackneyed outburst so wrongly apt that it should have been collated by lexicographers then and there and included in compendiums of mis-fitting expostulations.

'That cannot be true!'

26

But it was true. Damian wanted to caper and gibber, pinch himself, slap himself, swoon or do a succession of double takes, like in an old comedy film. He read the board over and over, taking in every detail. He wanted to take it home with him, a souvenir he could put in his room to prove he'd been here but it was firmly fixed, so he read it again and again.

It described one of the country's oldest folk traditions: The Haxey Hood, which went back to the fourteenth century and commemorated an event where the wife of a John de Mowbray was riding across the hill when a gust of wind took off the silk riding-hood she was wearing and blew it away across the fields. Thirteen locals chased after it and one of them got his hands on the hood, but being too shy to give it to the fine lady himself, he gave it to one of the others to hand over. She was happy to get it back and had said that the one who'd got it first had acted like a fool for not giving it to her in person and the one who had given it to her had acted like a lord, so she donated thirteen acres of her land to the parish with the instruction that every year they should re-enact what had happened in the form of a game on the day it happened, the 6th January, the Feast of the Epiphany, Three Kings day.

Every unbelievable detail was to be relished. This wasn't chutney, no sir. The game was preposterously authentic and had taken place every year since it had started. You could have made it up but you didn't have to because history had already done that for you and the details were mouth-watering. He drooled.

There was a 'Lord of the Hood' who was the referee and he had twelve 'bogggins' under him, who were like safety marshals, and there was a 'Fool'. Midday on the 6th January they all go round the four parish pubs singing three songs in each: 'Farmer's Boy', 'John Barleycorn', and best of all, 'Drink Old England Dry', boozing all the while, he assumed. After that, they go to a special place on the churchyard wall where the Fool makes a speech over a burning pile of smoky damp straw. Apparently he used to be held upside down over it but there had been an accident one year. The Fool starts the game off with a special proclamation in local dialect which sets out the basic guidelines:

'House against house, town against town, if you meet a man, knock him down, but don't hurt him.'

Then come some children's games where they chase pretend hoods made of tightly-rolled sacking and if they can get it to a pub they earn some money, nice to keep the kids involved from an early age, then comes the real game. It used to be played with an ox's head but the modern 'hood' was a two- foot leather truncheon. You weren't allowed to throw it or run with it. You had to sort of pull it around, or 'sway' it all over the place until it got to the door of one of the pubs and if the landlord could touch it without leaving their own step, it would belong to them for the year, until the next game. Anybody could pile on and the boggins went around trying to keep damage to a minimum.

The Lord and his boggins all seemed to wear red tops. Damian just knew that red was the colour of the original hood, not because it was a riding-hood, but because he was sure that Romana had made him come here because that's what she'd been wearing in his vision.

Damian was reverberating. He needed to have a sit down so he could take it all in and headed back towards his car, changing his mind on the way, and going round the church again, prior to coming back to the panel to read it for the last time. Romana had done him a big favour. She'd given him the idea of using tomb effigies by insinuating herself into his vision and mutating it so that he saw her looking on, and the effigy-like body, at the same time, so thanks Romana, that idea had been critical. She'd also brought him here to Mowbrayland to discover an authentic folkloric relic of an earlier age which she was maybe connected to.

Damian would have liked to meet Mowbray but he didn't have an effigy so wasn't on the agenda, maybe there was a plaque or something in Venice. There were nice views around the church but it seemed to have had a lot of its medieval detail restored away in the nineteenth century, unless it had always been a bit dull.

'Romana, you have been busy!' Amidst the plainness of the church, one decoration was set all by itself above a side-chapel window. He'd missed it before, a much-weathered stone head. 'Is that why I'm here?' But was it Venice Thomas Mowbray, Battle of Shipton Thomas Mowbray or was it John, Shipton Thomas Mowbray's brother? Or another? It was getting a bit fanciful, a bit legendary, but Damian knew Romana's game. She'd wanted to show him how to get into the story because she wanted the story to come out; she'd unlocked it for him and he was grateful. It was time for Damian to prove his mettle. No easy return to Epsilon Precinct and soft living for him but on, on to Norwich, whatever the cost.

It was too late to get to Norwich cathedral in time that day. It was probably four hours away and out of the question. He could pootle down there, lay up in a bolt hole somewhere and wait for tomorrow. Sleeping in a car overnight was no problem this time of year and he'd done it a couple of times before. Supermarkets were open late and he could buy some cheap shirts and stuff, and a few other things, and you had what you needed. Getting there was straightforward enough and he had time to drive around in the evening and see some interesting local things, which he did, sticking his nose into where Nelson lived, seeing the pond in the shape of a warship he'd dug when he was bored, and picnicking at Bacon Castle.

Eventually it was late, time to kip, and he found an unobtrusive place to park up and get some shut-eye. Nights were short and he snoozed well for a few hours but woke far too early. It was technically morning but still effectively night-time. He would make a move and go and see the sea. Fifteen minutes later he was in a boatyard car park landing-place by a salt-marsh waterway and hoped he hadn't woken anybody in the nearby houses as everything he did seemed very loud when he got out of his car. The dawn was chasing the dark and lighting the early-morning clear blue sky, silhouetting the anchored dinghies, marshes and distant sea and turning the river silver as a wash of red and orange coloured the horizon. Very soon the sound of steel cables tinking against metal masts was drowned by sea birds cawing and croaking to each other in a growing cacophonic din as if taking part in a daily shrieking contest where extra marks are awarded for dissonance. How could anybody sleep around here with that noise going on every morning? No wonder he'd not woken anyone up; they were all used to it.

Damian got back in his car. 'Enquiry' seemed to lack something; what he was doing was more important than that, more like a quest. He was really getting into it. What did you call it when a dog found something by smelling it out? Sniffing? Sleuthing? What was the word for when you were doing what he was doing? He pictured a black spaniel searching a meadow of flowers and grasses, its tail showing above like a waving ostrich feather, going round in wide circles, doubling back, changing direction, sometimes going the wrong way but always, always, nearing what it was looking for until, there it is, he's on top of it, some snuffles, some snouting and bang he's got it. And here he comes bounding back with it in his mouth. Good boy! What was the word for that? Was it dogging? Given his impromptu overnighting, it shouldn't be that. Too ambiguous. He was sniffing out the head honcho. The dog's name was Jack. Jacking. Jackusing. Too far-fetched. Quest was highfalutin. Enquiry would have to do. That would be fine. Still a long time to go. What about more shut-eye and kip, then to a garage early-doors for coffee, then Norwich, stooge around a bit, find an early-opening café, paper et cetera, a wander, then in? But too noisy here. Damian drove off and found another quieter temporary refuge and lay in wait.

27

Norwich offered two interview opportunities: with Bishop Despenser via his wooden head on a folding chair in the cathedral and with Sir Thomas Erpingham, via his statue above a gate outside.

These two had had a bad relationship although they shared certain traits like fighting and killing peasants. They had also both supervised the hanging, drawing and quartering of opponents and didn't seem to mind it, especially Erpingham, who quite enjoyed it; he had infamously mocked Sir Thomas Blount as he was having his stomach cut open at Oxford in the Epiphany Rising.

There were similarities but they were on different sides. The loyal bishop was serving with two-faced Edmund of Langley, Duke of York, when Henry's rebel army, on its dash for the crown, met them between Gloucester and Bristol. The grand old duke changed sides on the spot without a pike being wagged but the bishop had wanted to fight on and was overruled. This marked his card and he was implicated in the Epiphany Rising 4 months later. Some people had wanted him dead, including Erpingham, but he was lucky, saved by his surplice. His nephew, Thomas Despenser, wasn't. This was a colourful story, but not central, so he would leave seeing the bishop's face on a misericord for another time and dispense with Despenser.

But Erpingham? Erpingham was quite another matter

entirely. At one point it had seemed that Erpingham had been at the heart of the story but Damian's opinions about this had changed. He'd also despised Erpingham for his blood lust, but this view had changed as well. He saw him now more as a professional, one of a new class of full-time soldiers, who were good at their jobs and that's how they'd got on in life, making their living as mercenary adventurers, looking for action and thereby wealth in an age of chivalry for the top dogs and cruelty for the rest. Erpingham was fascinating.

A very long life, he basically outlived them all, dying in 1428 at the unfeasibly old age of 73. He'd done everything; thirteen when he started his career as a soldier with the Black Prince and John of Gaunt in France, he joined Big John's personal retinue in 1386 for the Spanish expedition, when Henry was left behind, and then became directly associated with Henry IV from 1390 on. A famous commander at Agincourt, he left soldiering, soon after, around 1416, giving himself a twelve-year retirement.

Erpingham had given the cathedral an enormous sum of money, maybe all that he'd had, which they'd used to finance building work, including the gatehouse named after him. His statue is up in a niche over the gate, on its knees, beseeching, an old man in armour, begging for mercy, looking pathetic. The gate had a legend to it, something to do with Erpingham and some monks and some killing. Lingering in the myth was the trace of an historic enmity between him and the church. And death.

Well, Erpingham had tried to get the bishop killed, so there was some truth there. At the end of his life, guilt had come to him and he'd tried to buy himself out of sin. His actual tomb was inside the cathedral, a box-chest tomb with no effigy. Had he made enough money to redeem himself? Damian could have chatted with Erpingham for hours but there was only one subject that Damian wanted to go over with him.

'Erpingham, I've come for your story'. Damian thought he'd go in hard, show the old git that he wasn't to be messed with.

'Magic word?'

'The magic word is please.'

'Put it in a sentence!' The old git was playing him.

'Erpingham, I've come for your story, please.' Erpingham had taken back control.

'You know a lot already. Is it my repentance you want to talk about or do you want to mock me for hypocrisy?'

'Neither, it's about Henry IV. It's about Prussia.' Erpingham didn't want to talk about Prussia.

'You know, I was Gaunt's man first, that was my best time and what a lord he was. I wish he'd kept me with him. He should have kept me with him.'

'Why didn't he?'

'Because he trusted me to do a good job.' Damian knew this too. When he'd been trying to get a handle on what Erpingham was like, he'd begun to compare him to a character in an American T.V show called Mike. Mike was a fixer for the less-bad crime bosses. He could do everything well, coolly, and with aplomb; breaking in, shooting, covering up. Always level-headed, dependable, with his own code of loyalty and conduct. The Duke had needed a Mike to keep his son Henry out of trouble, so he got an Erpingham.

'What kind of trouble?'

'Any kind.' Erpingham had a gravelly, drawly voice.

'So why did John of Gaunt need someone like you?'

'Because the Duke wanted Henry out of the country and somewhere else where he couldn't cause any trouble or, if he did, it could be covered up, by me, with nobody getting to hear about it. So the dust he'd raised back home could settle.'

'You were his bodyguard and you went to Prussia?'

'If that's what you want to call it then sure, I was his bodyguard. The Duke gave Henry a lot of money and told him to get himself lost, and he gave me special instructions. Yes, me and my team took Henry to Prussia on a crusade and we kept him out of the way there for nearly a year. August 1390 to April 1391, OK 9 months if you're being pedantic.' If Erpingham hadn't been a statue, he would have shot Damian a defiant look.

'Then what?'

'Henry was getting hard to handle so the Duke kicked him out again, gave us more money and we took him off to Prussia again.'

'When was that?'

'July 1392 to June 1393.' A full year this time, thought Damian.

'That was a longer trip.'

'Sure it was. It seemed never ending. Problem was that they didn't want him back in Prussia. Their one time with Henry had been enough for them. "Keep walking kid", they said to him and we had to keep on going.'

'Where'd you get to?'

'Everywhere. Prague, Vienna, down to Venice, then Dalmatia, Corfu, Rhodes, Jaffa, Jerusalem, Cyprus, Venice again, Padua, Milan, Paris. It was quite a year. I was busy all the time. All the time. There's a lot that can go wrong on a complicated itinerary like that, but I was well looked after by the Duke. He was very grateful. I made a lot of money.'

'Then what happened?'

'I disbanded the team of course, we were all on retainers anyway so we were, so to speak, furloughed. Not a problem, we'd been away a long time and had business to take care of in England and there were always little jobs going in any case.'

'Little jobs?'

'Yeah, like, you know, "the Duke is going up North, needs a pair of eyes", that kind of thing.'

'Any big jobs?'

'Not really.'

'Sure?'

'Sure I'm sure'. A pause.' Well, not until the big job came along.'

'Which big job was that?'

'Sit with Henry whilst he's in exile, look after him, keep him, you know, "well" and out of trouble.'

'When was that?'

'1398. The Duke wanted Henry out of the way, permanently.'

'You were going to bump him off?'

'No. You're so green, The Duke's patience with Henry was at an end. They were chalk and cheese. He was a stone in the Duke's shoe. Sometimes you'd think that Henry was trying to get under the Duke's skin on purpose. The Duke had had enough and wanted him gone in exile for a long time. It was the way out for everyone. I didn't really want the gig. It wasn't my style, a long term sit and, anyway, I'd had enough of his company. More than enough. But I had an offer I couldn't refuse.'

'Cash?'

'Yep. A lot. So then the Duke dies and now it's all up in the air. I didn't like that. I like to know what's going on. I had to figure things out with no Duke pulling the strings. Henry made a come-back plan and so we were back in play. I enjoyed this one more. It was like the old days with the Duke. Marching, fighting, being one-up because, you know, we were the best, me and my team and we were back, in action again.'

'Like with Blount?'

'Yes. I had orders.'

'Like killing 29 prisoners in the Green Ditch at Oxford?' Damian had been to Oxford and walked up Broad Street but hadn't known that it covered the site of this ditch of death.

'Yeah, I had orders. I got right into it. I wanted to show who's team I was on.'

'Like when you said that Richard should be offed?'

'I've just told you, haven't I?' I've just told you all that. I told you.' A strident tone, exasperated. 'Yes. I was on the team and a lot of it was my team anyway, my old team.'

'So what got you cheesed off with the project?'

'After a couple of years I was wondering, you know: where do we go from here? There was a new king but so what? We'd lost a lot along the way putting him there, like the rules of the game had been thrown away, and I didn't like the new rules. I knew I'd been part of the problem. I began to see the blood and the glory started to stink rotten.

It got better with Henry V. He was, you know, stuck in it like me. He didn't really want it, but had to keep it or get liquidated, and get everyone else liquidated. I felt the same. It was go on or go under. He was a good kid: ideals, honour – the works – like his grandfather. I was proud to serve him.

I did a good job at Agincourt but, you know, so what, anybody could tell that we were never going to beat France in the end. But we had to keep fighting to keep things together our end. I was happy to help and I did a good job, but piling up the bodies wasn't what I was into any more. Agincourt was the end. I felt used.'

'You felt used?'

'I was used. I was good at doing what I did. I got things done.'

'And after Agincourt?'

I came back here. I had a lot of things to put right. The Bishop was dead. Too late to sort that one out. I gave what I had to the church.'

'How did it go?'

'Sonny, I'm still up here praying; you work it out.'

Damian had what he needed and it was time to make his excuses and leave. He'd practised several parting shots which reflected how he'd been thinking about Erpingham but Damian hadn't settled on one he felt did him justice. First on the menu had been a couple of vulgar hand signals, then there was a simple turn of the back followed by a passive-aggressive walkaway, which would have been good, dignified. Various combinations had been rehearsed but Damian had distanced himself from judgementality and went for the rigorously formal:

'Thank you for your time Sir Thomas. I must leave now. Goodbye.'

'Goodbye.'

It had ended up more like a no-blame truth and reconciliation testimony-taking. Erpingham was a man of his times looking for a way up, a careerist in the newly professionalised armed forces of the day. No space anymore for walk-ups with just a rusty knife and a leather jerkin looking to join the feudal rabble of pomposity they called an army for a good per diem. Those days were over. From Erpingham on you needed a c.v. and the right kind of experience. Damian blamed society. It was still early, where to next? Could he make Canterbury? There was one way to find out.

28

Canterbury's streets pullulated with foreign teenagers being shepherded around by their teachers and other responsible adults; an urban scenario which inhibited Damian's deployment of his purposeful stride so, adapting his crowded-pub weaving techniques, he darted through them like a spirited rugby player and made a skillful dash for the cathedral.

Sleeping in the car had been adventurous, a dynamic and opportunistic response, but he was now feeling the lack of a comfortable bed and a good night's sleep and foresaw a cheerful hostelry somewhere with simply-furnished accommodation at reasonable prices to end the day with, after a decent meal. A slight dullness up top might be no bad thing, as it was time to confront the monster itself, and it might help to suppress his nerves. The wide arcade entrance of an empty shop provided a shelter from the busy streets and a chance to take stock.

He would need to characterise his role, inhabit it and not quail in front of the uncommonly ambitious parvenu that was Henry, so-called 'the Fourth': thief of majesty, robber of royalty, cat-burglar of crowns and spin-doctor of deceit extraordinaire versus honest Email of the Carabinieri, whose training, cunning, obsession with Truth and scrupulous objectivity made him, Commandatore Email, nicknamed: 'Gimlet', the ideal interrogator for this criminal lunatic. Envelope in hand, Damian devoured the details, wishing he had a hangover to add to his fatigue.

There he was, Henry the Fourth, be-robed and be-crowned, next to Queen Joan of Navarre. The male figures in full armour were the most interesting in the early days but as his tastes became sophisticated he found himself being drawn more to the female figures. Armour was just armour. The female costumes were more varied and better reflected the particular tastes and ambitions of their owners, but he wasn't here for Joan, so ignored her finery; she didn't look like a devotee of witchcraft yet she'd been prosecuted for it and Henry V had been her protector.

Both she and Henry were missing their hands, guilty hands holding rosaries, as they'd been taken off by state-licensed iconoclasts. Henry and Joan had hoped to count their rosary beads together, forever, to show how fervent was their religion, how sincere they were in their hope for mercy on doomsday. But someone else, equally fervently and sincerely, had put paid to their plan. No rosaries, no hands, how did they feel about it now?

Henry was the spitting image of Henry the Eighth, his face bearded, puffy and large. In 1831, antiquarians had opened a hole in his tomb, messed around with his body and said that yes, he did look like his effigy, and that he had auburn hair. Damian wondered if he still looked recognisable inside the stone tomb, or whether their intrusions had hastened the final decay of what was left of him. Well anyway, his remains were there and his effigy was on top of them. That's what counted.

Damian ran through the details, looking at his reflection in the shop window and making little theatrical movements, his mouth opening and closing, like an actor in rehearsal going over his lines and trying to 'find' the part.

'Am I looking at you? Am I looking at you? I must be because there's no one else here.' Damian squared up to his reflection and outfaced it, gimlet-eyes brooking no intimidation.

He had to think big. Be like 'Gimlet' Email of the Carabinieri, as at home in the courtroom as on Palermo's unforgiving streets. Gimlet got his name because he could see through the facts and find the key questions. There was a question that history avoided asking. It seemed trifling maybe, given the sensationalism in most of this story but why were historians so shy about asking it. Commandatore Gimlet Email was anything but shy, he was positively germanic when it came to getting to the point.

Why had Henry picked a fight with Thomas of Mowbray in December 1397 which brought exile on them both? Mowbray had been his fellow conspirator 10 years before. There had been a reckoning between king Richard and Henry's old gang but Henry and Mowbray had been left out of it, protected by powerful interests. Henry had deliberately provoked a show-down with Mowbray but hadn't needed to, as far as could be seen, so why did he?

Ready and in character, Damian got himself to the cathedral and went first to the Black Prince's tomb in the cathedral for a quick squizz at his hateful punky gloves, and then to Henry's to await a suitable moment, which soon presented.

'You are King Henry the Fourth.' Silence.

'I'll repeat the question. You are King Henry the Fourth.' Silence.

'We can do this the easy way, this way, or the hard way.' Silence.

'The hard way is I walk out of here right now. Right now! Which will it be?' Silence.

Commandatore Email's practised techniques hadn't brought quick results but he'd expected Henry to be a tough nut to crack and crack him he would, with special weapons and tactics; he needed a tool like the one you use to open oysters, or an awl, Or a gimlet. He would try again.

'I don't need your testimony Henry. I've got all I need. I don't actually want to be here. I don't need it. I've got plenty. I've been sent here by head office. I told them don't bother. He's a murderous usurper with a personality disorder trying to put it all behind him and be forgiven. We don't need him. How's it going with that by the way, the forgiveness? What did they do to your hands, chop 'em off?'

Damian was on a roll.

'By the way, Erpingham squawked and spilled the beans. He sang like a canary.' Damian left it hanging a few seconds. It wasn't his style to be nasty but he had to be taken seriously. He'd softened him up a bit. Now was the time to bad cop him – turn the tape off and rough him up a bit.

'They say that your son Henry the Fifth loved Richard more than he loved you.' He let the words settle on the stones to be taken up by them like water on a sponge.

'Say that again!' threatened a well-bred voice with a rich timbre which could have belonged to a menacing home-counties Richard Burton.

'You heard me cloth ears. I said that Henry loved Richard more than he loved you.' The bogus king was not to be drawn, but yet was.

'No comment.'

'Richard was like a father to him.'

'No comment.'

'And you were like a brother to Richard, you were knighted together, lived in the same household for a time and shared the same tutor, Simon Burley.'

'Burley was my tutor for a time.' Damian began a smirk and suppressed it, he'd got through. There were buttons you could push.

29

'You married Mary de Bohun in 1380, you were both very young, weren't you?'

'Yes.'

'This Mary was heiress to the Earl of Hereford's fortune and his title. Mary had a co-heiress, her sister Eleanor, and the Earl was already dead. There were opportunities to be had. There are some questions about how you managed to get your hands on her, aren't there?' Silence.

'Let me go on then. She had to be abducted from a nunnery, didn't she?'

'Yes, we used to joke about it.'

'What was she doing there?'

'Learning to be a nun.'

'You know what I'm talking about.'

'Thomas of Woodstock, my father's younger brother put her in one because he'd married Eleanor and wanted the whole fortune for himself.'

'Who organised your marriage to her?'

'Her mother, Joan Fitzalan, planned it and my father, John of Gaunt supported and financed some of it, I believe.' Damian was doubtful, John of Gaunt was out of the country at the time, but it might have been true.

'Joan was one of the rich and powerful Arundel family, wasn't she? Where did the marriage take place?'

'Mary was taken to Arundel castle and I met her there. We got married there.'

'John of Gaunt's brother, what was his name again?'

'Thomas of Woodstock, I told you that.'

Damian paused and pictured Woodstock at the time of the wedding, 25 years old, John of Gaunt's younger brother by 15 years, fuming and bashing a table with his leather-clad fist, 'Drat! Drat! And double-drat! Curses! Foiled again,' before picking up from where he'd left off.

'You, Woodstock and the Arundels all kissed and made up though, didn't you?'

'It wasn't personal. It was business, so yes, if you like.' It was time to move it on, Henry was hooked; could he land him?

'Did you ever rebel against the king of England?'

'No comment.'

'I'll repeat the question, maybe you didn't hear me?'

'No.'

'You never rebelled against the king of England.'

'Yes. That's correct.'

'Let's take it step by step then. Your new best friend Thomas of Woodstock threatened the king with being taken off his throne in the so-called Wonderful Parliament of October 1386, a couple of months after John of Gaunt left you behind in Plymouth, waving your hanky.'

'I can't remember.'

'Is that how we do things in England? An over-mighty noble can bully a king off his throne.' Silence.

'Richard III and Thomas of Lancaster both died in Pontefract castle. One in 1400 and the other in 1322. Did you vengefully put Richard in the same room that had been used for Thomas because you were self-consciously working out a better ending for Thomas's rebellion against Edward II all those years ago?'

Facts were thin on the ground, but it was possible that they'd both awaited their fate in the same cell; they'd definitely died in the same castle. From what we know of Henry's character, could it have even been likely? Had he engineered a cruel coincidence? Was it an opportunity for sweet vengeance that was not to be missed? Was it a dish served very cold? Some would have enjoyed it.

Silence again. Commandatore Gimlet Email chanced a low provocation.

'You waved John of Gaunt, his army, and your sisters, off with a big white hanky from the quayside at Plymouth, did you not?'

'I can't remember.'

'Was it maybe not a hanky, but more of a blouse, or shirt then?' Silence. It didn't seem to be an issue of terminology or precision. Damian moved on.

'Do you remember the Battle of Radcot Bridge in December 1387?'

'I have some recollection, it was all a long time ago, it's very hazy.'

'Maybe I can help you out. You, the Earl of Arundel, Thomas of Woodstock, Thomas Mowbray and the Earl of Warwick got an army together to stop help getting to King Richard who was trapped in London and effectively a prisoner. You won the battle and then paraded in triumph through Oxford, you at its very front, leading the procession.' Silence. 'That's funny because you were the most active participant in that engagement. It's a historical fact.'

'We weren't rebels. The king was being badly advised by evil favourites. We wanted to protect him from them.'

'They all say that,' said Damian to himself, not wanting to show his hand, 'don't gaslight me scumbag,' and then firmly out loud:

'You were a full participant in the Merciless parliament of 1388 which followed.'

'I had every right to be there.'

'Why was it called "Merciless"?'

'We didn't call it that.'

'You fought against the king in 1387 and then took over his government for, what, about a year?"

'We wanted to protect the realm from the depredations of evil counsellors and we did so.'

'Did you and your coterie of sanctimonious self-serving noble thugs become evil counsellors yourselves?' Was this silence an annoyed one? Damian was annoyed with himself for straying over the line of impartiality and returned to the light. 'Twelve years between your first attempt to take power in 1387 and your successful one in 1399. That's a long time. Plenty of time to get your ducks in a row, if that's what you wanted.'

'I don't understand what you're talking about. Everything we did was for the good of the country, I do assure you.'

'OK Henry, No further questions. That's all.'

'Good day to you.' Now it was time to get the fish in the net with a classic gambit.

'Oh, one more thing,' Damian rubbed his temple as though trying to summon up a mental shopping list and work out which insignificant item that his wife had asked for had slipped his mind then saying sotto voce 'Why did you pick a fight with Mowbray?'

'What?'

'Yes Henry the Fourth, one more thing, I nearly forgot, it must have slipped my mind. Why did you pick a fight with Mowbray?' Damian wanted a 'You want the truth? You can't handle the truth!' blurting, followed by a full and self-condemnatory exposition but answer came there none, so he had to go onwards and inwards.

"You picked a fight with former gang-banger Thomas Mowbray and wanted him out of the picture, one way or another. The story put about, maybe by you, is that one day in December 1397 you were out riding with him and he told you that there was a plot to kill you and John of Gaunt at Windsor. You provided a list of these 'conspirators' and, surprise surprise, they all wind up dead two years later when you sort them out.' Damian listed the victims after a dramatic caesura 'Epiphany Rising: John Holland, Duke of Exeter, Thomas Holland, Duke of Surrey, William Scrope, Earl of Wiltshire and John Montagu, Earl of Salisbury, killed at Bristol with Bussy, Bagot and Green when you eliminated Richard's loyalists.'

'Funny how all the plotters winded up dead, isn't it? It's funny how all the dukes and earls that Richard made ended up dead, except you and the Duke of Aumerle, Edward of Norwich, the son of the two-faced Duke of York. Richard gave all you new dukes and earls a massive party and your sister Elizabeth won the prizes for being the best singer and the best dancer. Go girl! But all the dukes and earls end up dead within two years, or five if you're lucky, like the Earl of Worcester.' Still no sound.

'John of Gaunt told you to drop it when you told him about the plot but you wouldn't listen and went straight to King Richard and accused Mowbray of treason. Richard said drop it, but you wouldn't and insisted it go to parliament but you couldn't get them to back you. They told you to drop it. Nobody took it seriously. Nobody took you seriously, so you had to accuse Mowbray in a court of chivalry, a sort of private court of honour. A bit rich Henry, no? A court of chivalry? Ironic, no?

And then you wanted a great big set-piece tournament to the death to sort it out. Trial by combat. Let God decide. Timetabled for September 1398. Nine months in the making. You really wanted to make it happen, didn't you? What a show-down! What an anti-climax more like! You're both there, suited and booted, he in armour from Milan that took 4 months to make and you in armour from Prussia that took 4 months to make. That's fair. You're all horsed-up, lances couched, ready to charge each other down. But wait! Oh no!'

Damian was enjoying this, accentuating, using tone and effects, bulging his eyes, raising his hands, properly camp.

'It's over before the start. Groans and moans from the stands. The king signals the tournament to stop and it's back to the bench for both of you.'

Damian didn't know why Henry was so fixed on pursuing this vendetta against Mowbray and historians weren't over-bothered to find out. Cancelling the tournament at the very last moment was made out to be another example of Richard's fickle and unworthy nature, but there must have been more to it, after all; John of Gaunt would have been there himself. Maybe a straightforward binary tournament outcome would have left some political problems behind and that exiling them both was the only solution; if Mowbray killed Henry, that was John of Gaunt's son and most legitimate heir gone for good. If Henry killed Mowbray, that was Richard's new best friend dead and troublesome Henry still hanging around to mischief-make. Damian suspected that it was John of Gaunt who pulled the strings and came up with the expedient exile solution as way out of the political cul-de-sac.

'So why did you pick a quarrel with Mowbray?' This was harder than he'd thought.

'No comment.'

'Your old gang was a bit broken up, wasn't it? Thomas of Woodstock was murdered, the Earl of Arundel was executed, Warwick was in the Tower or exiled to the Isle of Man, I forget which. It was only you and Mowbray left, and Mowbray had been working his way back into royal favour. Him gone would have left you as the last man standing.'

'No comment.'

'You wanted him dead.' Silence.

'Is there anything you want to tell me?'

'I hope you get sick and die.'

Damian would have been thrown by the goading explicit viciousness but not so the Commandatore. Henry had been stricken with disease soon after taking the throne and his face had been polluted by retributive excrescences. Everyone gets sick and dies. It was an empty threat.

'Ok king, we're done here. No further questions.'

He'd given him his chance. Silence was no defence against facts. The commandatore had the evidence anyway. It would have been nice to have got more but the quarrel question was not strictly speaking germane to the prosecution's case, it was more for his personal satisfaction; Gimlet liked the 'T's and 'I's crossed and dotted. No loose ends.

30

Damian was happy to use Chichester as a short-term base of operations, the hotel he'd found had been okay, not at all modestly priced, but the only one with accommodation available to walk-ups at that time of year. His room was pokey and over-heated, typical of the overnight rip-offery ubiquitous in sought-after locations when you were a bit desperate, he moaned briefly, before getting himself a pretty good meal round the corner in a pub with some goodly ale and goodly reading matter. He'd furtled around the town, had a pint or two in a friendly Irish bar, and returned nourished, restored and sleepy.

The breakfast had been digestible and the coffee unusually decent for a hotel. Today would be a big one. 'Big one' was an unsatisfactory description so, taking his cue from Dolmetscher's exhortation to loosen up his vocabulary, he sought a better and more apposite description for this day of days, and found one; it would be his apotheosis. If he played his cards right he could see all the rest of his enveloped effigies today, starting with the Arundel tombs in the castle and then to London by train to see Richard II in Westminster Abbey.

That would leave him a couple of days to write up his enquiry and the job would be done to the deadline. A tight schedule surely but the tiniest of digressions was available for gisant in Chichester cathedral was Richard Fitzalan, the 3rd Earl of Arundel, and his wife, Eleanor of Lancaster, who were waiting supine for the end of time, hand in hand. John of Gaunt and Blanche had been portrayed holding hands on their tomb as well, as was their daughter Phillipa and her husband in Portugal. Maybe the 3rd Earl had set a trend? It was touching. They weren't witnesses as such, just the parents of some key actors but Eleanor linked the Arundels to the Lancasters; Henry IV and the bad 4th earl of Arundel shared a bloodline back to unlucky Thomas of Lancaster of Boroughbridge and it wouldn't hurt to see them both in the cathedral before driving up the road to Arundel.

Studying the picture on his information envelope, Richard Fitzalan, evidently a most noble and chivalrous knight, was recumbent in full armour next to his wife, each holding the other's right hand, she slightly turned towards him with her right leg overlying her left. He is dressed for war and she is dressed most meekly, more like a nun than a grand lady of one of the country's richest families; a family wealthy enough to lend to ever-needy kings. A family that's going to make an alliance with another branch of the Lancasters and make a move on the throne when Richard and Eleanor are dead.

Damian had found a poem by Phillip Larkin called 'The Arundel Tomb' about this pair and he took out the copy he'd made from their envelope. She'd died 5 years before him so it had been Earl Richard who had ensured the tomb was as it was. Damian had seen from internet images that the Earl's feet rested on a lion and it looked as if Eleanor's feet were resting on a sheep, so where was the dog that Larkin talked about in the first verse of the poem? Damian concluded that Larkin could only have seen a badly-printed and blurry photograph of their tomb and hadn't been there at all before writing it. The last line of the poem was famous: 'What will survive us is love'. He would see the real thing for himself. First visitor of the day, he sidled up to the statues.

'Tell him to go away,' said a quiet female voice, firmly.

'I will dear. Go away!' came a stern male command. Damian looked around but there was no one there. 'Go away! We will have nothing to do with you. Please leave.'

Damian made his french 'bof'; eyebrows raised, mouth turned down in a moue-ing 'I know nothing' pout, shoulders hunched, palms open.

'Don't pretend that you're not thinking about that terrible so-called poem by that famous let-down miserabilist poet-man. We know you are and we'd like you to go right now. Please go, you're upsetting her.'

Damian de-boffed but kept the quizzical look on his face.

'They're always coming here pestering us. We're not here for them, we're here for our maker to behold, to see the purity of our hearts, and our love. This is me, knight of chivalry, loyal servant of my king and this is my lady fair-o, queen of my heart so go and gawk at something else.'

That earl was a right softie, despite the armour but Damian took the hint and turned away, pretending that he had just casually found himself at their tomb for no particular reason and could just as easily find another place to be, having better things to do anyway and not needing the aggravation, sauntering off and almost muttering under his breath. He heard the woman again, presumably Eleanor.

'Is he gone?'

'Yes, dear.'

'Thank you for dealing with him Richard darling.'

'I will always be here, for you, now please try to get some rest.'

Damian's appetite for spending time in the cathedral was abruptly gone. He'd expected more of a welcome and felt piqued and indignant. He exited and found an outside wall to lean on while he processed the experience and took out the folded poem to read it again and quickly sympathised with the two of them. The poem was flat and dull. It made the obvious, obvious. The second verse said you get a 'sharp tender shock' when you see they are holding hands as if it comes at you by surprise. That was wrong. It was the most obvious part of the whole thing. You couldn't miss it.

And what's with: 'and with that faint hint of the absurd – the little dogs under their feet'?

One: why would dogs under their feet be absurd. They were commonly used to symbolise loyalty.

Two: there are no dogs there, one is clearly a lion, courage, strength and resurrection and the other looks more like a sheep, or more likely a lamb; innocence maybe – or biblically 'the lion shall lie down with the lamb'? And if they were dogs so what, what's comical?

Damian knew a particular dog who probably had the soul of an Aryan prince that was steadily working its way back up the chain of reincarnations and had got this far. Or maybe an Aryan princess in a male dog body? Was it a spectrum? It didn't matter. That dog had a noble character. Damian thought Larkin over-rated anyway and if Larkin was the nation's best-loved poet or our greatest post-war poet, as some said, then lord save and protect us from the bad ones. What endured of the poem wasn't love at all. The poem was just an overwrought preamble to the oh-so-clever and memorable last line and lacked real feeling. Wordsworth would have spurned it. It was the last line that endured because it was facile. It was a phoney poem. Should he go back in and try and explain things? He didn't want to risk a second drubbing so got back to his car, drove to Arundel and parked outside the castle gates, where he sat thinking himself into his next call.

31

The Fitzalan-Arundel clan-faction-affinity-gang were at the epicentre of this historical vortex-earthquake-maelström. Good Sir Richard, lovingly glad-handing his wife in Chichester cathedral was the chivalric knight par exellence and he had more than 10 children but it was those of his second wife, dear Eleanor, who counted, especially big bad Richard, the cantankerous and king-hating 4th Earl, executed 1397, and sly Thomas, Bishop of Ely, later Archbishop of Canterbury.

There was also Joan, mother of Henry IV's wife; the vengeful murderess of Katherine of Lancaster's husband, little bad John who crashed his boat and drowned after pillaging a nunnery near Southampton and Alice and Eleanor, who kept themselves to themselves.

These family trees always made Damian's head spin. They all had similar names down the generations and so were easy to mix up. It was clear that the top families married amongst themselves to get and keep fortunes. A good example was how the Arundels got their hands on the Hereford bundle. Gallant Sir Richard's sister, Alice, married the 5th Earl of Hereford but it didn't work out as he couldn't get an heir, no matter who he married. His younger brother became the 6th Earl and couldn't make an heir either so the earldom went to his nephew when he died, who was snapped up by vengeful Joan, getting the Arundels back in the game and Joan's daughter marries the up-and- coming wannabe future king Henry IV, who becomes Earl of Hereford.

Four years later, the Arundels get their claws into Thomas Mowbray by marrying off the bad 4th Earl's daughter Elizabeth Fitzalan to him in 1384, four years before the first round of treachery. It's wound up and ready to go. Untangling all this made Damian puff and wince but it he'd made it much easier for himself by writing it out on his envelopes, he thought, when he could read his own writing.

The Arundel faction was compact in terms of the headline players and exceedingly well-resourced, comprising in wealth order: Warwick, Arundel, Henry, Woodstock and Mowbray. The 4th Earl was executed for treason in 1397 and his brother the Archbishop was exiled. The Archbishop's fatherless nephew, the new 5th Earl, joined him in France where they plotted with Henry, exiled for stubbornness, in the Hotel de Clisson, Paris; it's now called the Hotel de Soubise and houses the national history museum.

Did he really have anything he needed to ask? The bad 4th Earl wasn't there. Executed traitors don't get nice tombs, or any usually, and getting into Arundel castle to see the 5th Earl and his wife in the chapel was going to be pricey. Could he do a Larkin here? Do it vicariously from a distance by remote-control? What could the nephew tell him that he wanted to know? The Bad Arundel and the Sly Arundel weren't available; he knew he was going to skip this one so he could get to London and talk to Richard the Second himself. Richard knew what the Arundel clan-faction-gang had been up to and would be keen to talk. Not like Henry. Not like, he predicted, the 5th Earl of Arundel, who also had a lot to hide.

Damian pulled out the envelope and studied how the weasely nephew, gaining rank and position by hanging on to the usurper's coat-tails, had petrified their wordly status for posterity. Beatrice of Portugal, his wife, had a most singular head-dress and hair-do. Very showy indeed. She was the illegitimate daughter of King John, the self-same king John of Portugal who was married to Henry IV's sister, another Phillipa. Small world in name terms.

The 5th Earl's effigy was also dressed in court robes almost exactly like Henry IV's, although the Earl's robes seemed longer. One of the repeated criticisms in history books was that Richard made the court too regal but Henry IV and the 5th Earl of Arundel clearly liked dressing up and playing the part. No hands either. Ok, that would do, last man standing was King Richard, get to London, see him, get home, job done, let's go.

32

Trains left Arundel for London regularly and he'd have an hour and a half to day-dream away before having to get over to Westminster Abbey on foot from Victoria station, which was another half an hour on top, he reckoned, leaving plenty of time for the return journey.

It seemed that the gods themselves were smiling on him, egging him onwards, and he wasn't surprised to find a spice called 'sumac', which he'd never heard of, in the section next to canned fish when he went to a supermarket for some shopping and tweet for the journey. That was a sign, surely? He would buy some chicken and would use that spice on it when he got home. Do it in the oven whilst watching TV. Have some authentic Italian beer from Burton-on-Trent with it, and a baguette. Best get the chicken on the way back in case it went off in the car when he was away. It might get too hot. Newspaper for the train. Everything was in order.

Train music was soporific. They used to have buffet cars with a bar in. One small can of beer would be enough to get you dozy while the train-lullaby rocked you.

Diddly da, diddly da, – pause…, pause…,
Diddly da, diddly da, – pause…, pause…,

The landscape whizzed by. Once he'd had to learn a poem by Robert Louis Stevenson about being on a train for a public recital: 'Faster than fairies, houses and ditches and witches' or something was how it went. He'd forgotten the words on the night but never the shame and embarrassment of failing on stage. He didn't blame the poem and still liked it.

Diddly da, diddly da, – pause..., pause...,
  Diddly da, diddly da, – pause..., pause...,

Did fairies move that quickly? Were they known for being speedy? Those grand and noble families, all related to each other; they must have been skilled oral communicators – not much else by way of stimulation: no newspapers, books, telly, radio, internet. Probably had good memories and talked a lot, always eager for news. Always talking about what was going on: insults to their honour and dignity, chances coming up to make useful liaisons, gossip, intrigue and rumour-mongering. They were probably very talkative people. Maybe they never shut up.

'Stop banging on about that, that was long ago!' someone would say but they'd keep banging on about it saying:

'It wasn't that long ago actually and by rights it should have come to me, and if it had come to me, as it should have done, then it would come down to you in time and you would be grateful but that as nobody is doing anything about it, they are laughing at us from behind their hands and who could blame them. More fool you!'

Diddly da, diddly da, – pause..., pause...,
  Diddly da, diddly da, – pause..., pause...,

Damian thought more about Henry IV's inheritance 'issues'. History had swallowed Henry's cover story hook, line and sinker. It was the supposed reason he came back from exile early in high dudgeon, because Richard had denied him his inheritance, he said. This was always left rather vague in the books, sort of skated over, the casus belli.

Henry had no right to the lands and titles as they weren't his to inherit, just like that, as if it was like private property nowadays. Nobles were the monarch's tenants-in-chief; they didn't own their land, they held them from the king and that was the system. Actually, the held them from the king – ahem you listening Henry? – by dint of loyalty. That was well known. If there was some kind of problem, like a rebellion, these lands could be taken away but there were long-established precedents and mechanisms whereby a naughty baron could lose them and then get them back by paying a fine or something.

In fact, that was the preferred option, most things boiled down to cash in those days. Payments of different kinds sorted everything out. In fact, their society was basically payments all the way down, no wonder Chaucer called it a venal age.

> Diddly da, diddly da, – pause..., pause...,
> > Diddly da, diddly da, – pause..., pause...,

Henry hadn't been really naughty for a long time. His dad was dead and he was a big noise in his own right. He only had a handful of exile years left and then all he had to do was kiss the royal ring and swear loyalty, probably seal the deal with some cash and he's back. It wasn't absolutely clear that Richard had disinherited Henry at all. Nobody wanted resentments festering down the talkative generations.

Was Henry worried about losing the Earl of Hereford portion? It had all came to him when Woodstock died or was rather murdered. There was murkiness here. Henry was a beneficiary of the death. Follow the money? Too speculative. Did he fear that the king would not accept a Duke of Lancaster and Duke of Hereford in the same person and that maybe a lot of people would agree with this. Those measly people and those measly city corporations and burgesses, not to mention the church, tended to dislike over-mighty barons and saw the king's justice as a protection. Maybe he was afraid of losing one of his titles. Maybe two dukes into one Henry didn't go.

Diddly da, diddly da, − pause..., pause...,
Diddly da, diddly da, − pause..., pause...,

Isn't it difficult to say that you are coming back from exile to claim your rightful inheritance from the king and, by the way, you've got an army with you, and whoops, the royal army has melted away because its leader is probably in cahoots with you and all the proper royal soldiers are in Ireland on manoeuvers. It's a funny way of going about it.

Henry landed at Ravenspur on the Yorkshire coast on 4th July 1399 with 3 ships and some men, 200-300 of them, and just over 3 weeks later he was basketing up heads to show them off in London after having captured Bristol castle and killing the loyalists there. He was a fast mover. That's how you won. Wang Chung knew that.

Henry had picked up support in the North from the Earl of Northumberland and the Earl of Westmoreland. Westmoreland-Neville was on the way up but Nothumberland-Percy was going down, but didn't know it yet. What was Percy thinking? Was it the inheritance cover story that made him support Henry? Same for Neville. It was impossible to believe. Percy rued the day but had been more than willing at the start, he'd personally helped put the crown on Henry's head. His son Harry Hotspur was killed in battle against Henry in 1403 and the old man himself was killed at Bramham Moor in 1408. Was it like thieves falling out over the spoils? His mother was Mary of Lancaster, sister of Eleanor who lies gisant in Chichester with her chivalrous husband, the 3rd Earl of Arundel. That was another connection to unlucky Thomas at Boroughbridge. It's a small world for the Lancaster-Arundels and Percys. As ye sow, so shall ye reap Mr Percy; thou wert greedy and not cunning enough.

Hotspur had the best chance of unseating Henry by linking up with Owen Glendower in North Wales but Henry had got to the key place first and destroyed him and his army before they could unite. Wang Chung knew all about that old trick. Glendower was interesting too. He'd studied law in London, fought under various leaders and had even been part of the Larkin-intolerant 3rd Earl of Arundel's household, maybe also the naughty 4th Earl's, maybe Henry's himself. Glendower was no Merlin of the mists; he had been a player and knew what was what.

> Diddly da, diddly da, – pause..., pause...,
>> Diddly da, diddly da, – pause..., pause...,

The scenery was changing, thickening with houses and villages, towns, houses, roads, then coagulating into brick terraces, embankments, cuttings, graffiti, industrial buildings, offices, other lines joining, other trains passing. It was thrilling.

Damian wondered if, after leaving the station, he would be

accosted by a character with a hard-luck story needing a small and specific amount of money to add to what they had already, to get a train ticket to Carlisle. It was always Carlisle. Or somewhere else really far away. It was a small sum and they desperately wanted to get there. They must have been able to sense him coming. You were only asked once. They must put a mark on you somewhere to make sure you weren't accosted again, otherwise you'd know it was just a made up story. The worshipful guild of London accoster-mongers must have strict rules to protect their business and ensure their continuing prosperity.

33

Damian was accosted by a guy with a travel-plans-thwarted journey-based sob story just outside the station and was glad to give him some money and get it over with. It used to be around 50p but had clearly been going up over the years. Damian did some calculating and worked out that 50p then was the same, relatively, as what he'd been asked for today. La plus ça change indeed although technically not change any more as you needed a note.

What would he be asked for a cup of tea? It wouldn't be 10p. Anyway they didn't want tea any more, it would be coffee. There was plenty of time and he wouldn't have to use the ruse he'd prepared on the train, just in case he was next in line in the queue and they were closing, to bribe his way into the Abbey. One and half times the minimum wage would be reasonable given that he just needed to be let in and wouldn't be long anyway. That's how things were done in London he knew, you had to grease palms. Samuel Pepys used to spend half his time giving out gloves with money in them.

Purposeful walk fully deployed for maximum effect; his footwear was so right for these cockney pavements and the satisfying sound of his steps dogged him, almost overtaking as he moved along, ringing out, blending in with the other purposeful pavement users. The give-away tourist map showed him how to get there and it couldn't be easier; it was Victoria Street all the way down. Seeing his fleeting reflection in the window of an Italian restaurant, Damian was reminded of both Romana and the song 'Concrete and Clay' and began to hum it going along.

You to me, luh la-luh la la la-luh la la
              And you to me luh la-luh la la la-luh la la

Something about never dying because you'd see the mountains crumble before you said goodbye. Was that what Romana was about? Love? Had he been too hard on Larkin? Did love endure through time as a soomaky transcendence of self? Romana, I will find you, he vowed. No. he wasn't in love with her, that would be absurd. Should he put a grim face on to show determination? There was no need, you could tell by the way he walked he was a man with a purpose. Effigy interrogation had, by and large, been a great success but this was the ne plus ultra: Richard II himself. How would he handle him? Best to be upfront from the start. Just let him talk and maybe guide him towards certain areas if he turned out to be one of those rambling types.

Westminster Abbey wasn't as informal an entry as the others had been but that was no surprise. Some queuing, no bribery needed. not a problem. It was to be expected and he was good at waiting. In fact, he enjoyed his wait to get into the Abbey as deferred gratification had been built into the system. Maybe it was a pity the queue wasn't longer. But then his turn came and he was in. The Abbey was packed with people and things to see but he was very focussed and identified the correct area to head for, and went there.

Damian found a nook to loiter in while he enveloped the upcoming encounter. Richard would be lying next to his first wife, Anna of Bohemia. Both of them were dressed simply. He looked more like a monk and she wore her long hair bare and unadorned. Their arms had been removed but he'd found out that it was due to vandalism not iconoclasm, as they'd originally been holding hands like the Arundels, not holding rosaries. A long latin inscription was inscribed on the chest part of the tomb and Damian had its translation with him:

> 'Sage and elegant, lawfully Richard II, conquered by fate he lies here depicted beneath this marble. He was truthful in discourse and full of reason: Tall in body, he was prudent in his mind as Homer. He showed favour to the Church, he overthrew the proud and threw down anybody who violated the royal prerogative. He crushed heretics and laid low their friends. O merciful Christ, to whom he was devoted, may you save him through the prayers of the Baptist, whom he esteemed.'

And Anna had one:

> 'Beneath a broad stone now Anna lies entombed; when she lived in the world she was the bride of Richard the Second. She was devoted to Christ and well known for her deeds; she was ever inclined to give her gifts to the poor; she calmed quarrels and relieved the pregnant. She was beauteous in body and her face was gentle and pretty. She provided solace to widows, and medicine to the sick. In 1394 on a pleasant seventh day of the month of June, she passed over. Amen'.

Nice inscriptions, moving. She had died and he'd had to marry again, a French princess far too young, which is where his woes stemmed from. No heir. They looked serene. It was time. Damian made his way to their part of the Abbey and approached cautiously.

'King Richard, may I disturb you, please?'

'If you're quiet and don't wake Anna then certainly you may. Come nearer so we might talk together.' Damian did as he was requested.

'You have a very nice tomb.'

'Yes, I like it too. Anna was here first and then Henry the Fifth got me out of that awful friary where they had me and put me here.'

'Did Henry the Fifth write that inscription for you?'

'Yes he did, we got on very well.' Damian was unsure how to broach the subject and wanted to show sensitivity, Richard being a murder victim and all.

'King Richard, do you know why I've come?'

'Usually people come to pity me, is that why? They usually just stand and stare but you seem more curious.' Damian presented his credentials, put his cards on the table and explained that Henry IV and his allies had come up with a story that had stuck for centuries and that Damian wanted to pull the story apart and find a greater truth, something more like what had actually happened. He told the King how he was depicted in the history books.

'So for example, you were fond of young Henry V and that is used as evidence of you having the mind of a child. They like you facing down Wat Tyler and his mob when you were 14, but after that they cut you no slack. You are vain, overweening, full of airs and graces, partial to favourites, and fops, and fatally vengeful.'

'They said that to my face when I was alive. They wouldn't let me reign and they wouldn't let me live.'

'Could you give me a statement to that effect, on the record?'

'Yes,' the king collected his thoughts and began, 'I did have what they called "favourites" but I called them loyal servants. In those days it was all about patronage, they didn't get much of a salary but you could add on manors, fees, rents and all that sort of stuff. My enemies hated my servants because they wanted all that I gave my people for themselves. All the stuff about me being puffed up is baloney. It was all about ceremony, rank, dignity and courtliness in those days and I did much prefer all that to war, which I hated. Those who opposed me thought they could get richer through war and they were supported by the Duke of Orléans' war faction in France. Who pays for war? The king. Who pays the king? The people. I wanted peace. The people wanted peace.

'John of Gaunt?'

'He wanted peace. Certainly he did.'

'Did you overtax the country?'

'Nobody likes paying taxes and every groat comes with a groan, as the saying goes. Edward III had bled the country white. The country had got poorer, things had got more expensive, there had been dearth and famine. Edward made the throne dependent on the rich nobles like Warwick and Arundel for money after exhausting the Italians and robbing the Jews. That gave them a power. I think I did overtax the people, but I had no choice. I couldn't let my enemies use

their money to gain power over the throne, power over me.
I had to tax the people.'

   'Thank you King Richard.'

34

Damian told Richard what television was and what a documentary was. 'And every time there is a documentary we see the Wilton Diptych...,'

'Yes, I loved that. We used it on the altar sometimes, if we were in a little castle chapel or a manor house, you know, somewhere a bit plain.'

'Well they show it on the television and then they rip into you with, "There's Richard, looking like a bit of a girl, pretending he can talk to God and look at the angels. Look, he's put them in his army, what a megalomaniac." That's how they always show it.'

'Put that way I can see there could be a misapprehension, may I give you another statement, on the record?' Damian was surprised by the king's lack of assertiveness.

'Sure King, go ahead.' King Richard the Second of England made a further oral deposition: -

'One, everybody talks to God, it's called prayer, and I took my devotions seriously as did, I trust, everyone in my household, or if not, I'll know the reason why.

Two, for some reason, every picture of me is made to look more wimpy every time it's restored. My skin gets paler, my lips more and more like rosebuds, my beard recedes. I'm made to look like a man-boy-girl-woman. That's not what I looked like. This effigy was done from life. It's more me.

Three, the angels wearing my badge, the white hart. I can see how that is misperceived, but at the time it was quite the normal thing to do. Liveries were absolutely in fashion and there wasn't one family, guild, fraternity or merchant who didn't want to have an official livery. All those London guilds wanted to become livery companies and they did. It started under Edward III and went on from there. I made a lot of them myself, like the Mercers. I made them a livery company in 1394. Everybody was doing it or wanted to do it.

Four, as for the angels, that was a bit over the top perhaps, but it was made abroad, maybe it was too showy for England. Anyway it doesn't matter because its symbolic. When two companies in livery meet they exchange tokens and badges to show love and friendship. Was it too much?'

'I'm not here to say but they always use it to show you as being a bit of a prat. What about your household soldiers, they say you had too many.'

'You know what happened to me. I needed a force that I could depend on in case they came at me in arms again. I don't think I had any more household knights and esquires than any other king, like Edward III for example. I did have a regiment of Cheshire archers. They weren't technically 'household', but they were in livery on a retainer. The people who used to push me around didn't like not being able to anymore.'

'What about the vengeance?'

'Vengeance? Don't talk to me about vengeance,' spat the king. Damian had touched a nerve.

'King Richard, I have to. It's what they say about you, that you were vengeful.' Damian heard a puff of air. Richard had apparently puffed out his cheeks and then expelled a mouthful of air. Was that a 'huff' or a 'puff'. It only happened once so it couldn't be both.

'OK, I'll give you another statement. There was never a band of treacherous traitors more vengeful than that foul gang of bullies. Start with the Peasants Revolt and you'll find that they treated them quite vengefully.'

'King Richard, they say that you liked to be vengeful on the peasants as well.'

'I was fourteen. I didn't like revolts, it was scary, but they didn't need any encouragement from me to put the peasants down without mercy. They didn't even ask me, just told me what they'd done in my name. There was vengeance enough for everybody and they were always vengeful. They killed my man Molineux at Radcot bridge when he got out of the river after being stuck in it, and his squire, and his boy servant. He was my captain and they murdered him with a knife. In cold blood after he climbed out.

Yes, I served them their just desserts in time, but how could you call that vengeance? Is justice vengeance? It was justice, long-delayed yes, but I had to be strong enough to act. I had to wait for the right time. Arundel was executed, Warwick was exiled, some people paid some fines. That was it. That was the full extent of my so-called vengeance, after all that they did to me.'

'They say you had Thomas of Woodstock murdered.'

'Why would I? He'd already made a detailed confession. I could have brought him back from Calais whenever I wanted and put him on trial and the outcome would have been forgone. No, it wasn't me.'

'So who was it?'

'Finger pointing for the murder, that was part of Mowbray and Henry's quarrel and I think that Henry turned Mowbray's ten-year exile into a permanent one when he got my throne by saying he had something to do with it but...,'

'But what?' Damian came skidding in too quickly.

'As I was saying, ...but when Henry did a so-called proper investigation into it, the men who got hanged for doing it said the guy who put out the "hit", was my uncle, Edmund of Langley, Duke of York, Thomas of Woodstock's own brother and brother to John of Gaunt. Nothing happened to him though.

'It's fishy alright.' Damian thought of Fredo being taken out of the game in 'The Godfather II' for jeopardising the family project. Sad but necessary.

'It's not just fishy, it's stinky too. That man York was "Keeper of the Kingdom", "Custodian of the Realm" for me when I was in Ireland at the end. He ruled England in my name, like a governor. York gave it all to Henry when he asked for it and left my loyal servants to be murdered in Bristol.'

'I know, it must have been a massive let down.'

'You know it. And who's idea was it for me to take my best army and number one men to Ireland, do you think?'

'I don't know.' Damian felt he was being pushed in the direction of saying the Duke of York but he'd not found conclusive evidence, although it would explain a lot.

'Three guesses who?' This was conjecturing too far and Damian wanted to get back to the two main points he wanted to go over.

'I'll leave it there, king Richard, if I may. Can you tell me something about the "Merciless Parliament"?'

35

'The Merciless Parliament, of course. Can I make another statement?'

'Please do.'

'The clue's in the name: "Merciless". A treasonous and thuggish bag of snakes, led by Thomas of Woodstock, cornered me in 1386 and threatened to take away my throne. They took over parliament and wanted to get rid of all my loyal servitors. Things were going too slowly for them and it was beginning to look like they might just have been acting illegally, so they got their men together and chased me into the Tower of London where they told me they were going to take my throne. My people were beaten back at Radcot bridge and couldn't help me.

They couldn't agree amongst themselves who would be king so they put me back in parliament and carried on their dirty business. They called themselves the Lords Appellant meaning the lords who were making accusations and that's what they did. They accused many and executed many: John Beauchamp of Holt, Burley, Barret, Salisbury, Usk, Blake and many more. England's most prestigious lawyers were exiled to Ireland en masse because Woodstock and his crew didn't like what they said about the legalities. I had no choice. I had to put up with it.

Oh yes, they couldn't get what they wanted so they said that this royal council ('House of Lords' thought Damian) was actually above common law and that it didn't apply to them.

What the hell do you call that? Forget Magna Carta. Forget royal prerogative. What the hell is that about when you make yourself above the entire law of the land? Thank God I could get Gaunt back a year after they butchered my courtiers. The country was sick of them and wanted them out so how's that for vengeance and bloodshed. How's that for using prerogative privilege above the law, illegally? And they accused me of that! They revelled in their power and lusted after death for those that opposed them. I was one of many.'

This was well documented but Damian was especially curious about the death of Sir Simon Burley.

'Why were they so set on killing Burley?'

'That is good one. That's a good point. Most people, if they are interested and come here, they don't even ask but you know a lot, don't you? They wanted them all dead. But they wanted Simon dead the most. Many begged for his life to be spared. I begged. Anna begged. Mowbray begged. Even the Duke of York begged. We all begged Thomas of Woodstock to show mercy but he wouldn't. He even came up to me and shouted calumnies into my face, in parliament, I felt his hot sour breath and spittle in my face, on my throne. I thought he was going to punch me off it. Even Arundel's brother the Bishop of Ely, acting as Chancellor, sitting on the woolsack, tried to get Burley's life spared. We all begged for mercy but none was shown.

'So why was he so set on his death?'

'I think you know why,' Damian hadn't actually thought about this and let the king continue as he tried to work out why. 'Simon Burley was a very, very well-respected Knight. Soldier for Edward III, the Black prince, for John of Gaunt.

Humble origins. Gained advancement through service and valour, a fine and chivalrous knight. Wonderful fellow. His reputation was second to none and he was my tutor, and Henry's for a time. Thomas wanted his death very much. John of Gaunt would have been livid.'

The answer hit Damian in the face like an ice-cream cone dropped by a seagull on an unsuspecting tourist, suddenly and surprisingly.

'Because he guided you on how to be a king'

'In one! He shoots, he scores. Bravo. Now you get it, don't you. They wanted to get my confessor too but he had some protection from the Church.'

'Yes I do, thank you. Lastly King Richard, could we go over some details of your actual dethroning. I know this must be hard for you but I just need to get everything straight in my mind. It's well known that you were tricked into being captured by…,' Damian checked his envelope 'Henry Percy, Earl of Northumberland, and then you were taken to the Tower, what happened then?'

'It's the easiest part to tell. It's just one word: lie. It was a lie, and a lie, and a lie and a lie. It was lie upon lie upon lie.'

'I'm sure it was but I'm going to need more detail please.'

'I was in a room. I saw no one. I saw only them. They would come in and shout at me. Then leave. Then come back and shout again. Over and over. I saw no one. I wrote nothing. I would not sign. They got tired of getting nothing out of me. They brought their own mob to London and called it a parliament but it wasn't one.'

'Could I have a moment please?' Damian needed to gather his thoughts. He recalled a statistic, 30%, or was it 40%, of the so-called MP's had never been to parliament before. It had been a 'parliament' packed with the Henry's supporters, more an assembly; at the time it had been called a meeting of the 'estates', like a hand-picked mob you wanted to get a massive cheer from when they were asked 'Who wants Henry for King?'

'Ok, please go on.'

'They told that mob that I had willingly given up the throne. Lie. That it was vacant. Lie. That I had said I wasn't king anymore. Lie. That serpent Archbishop Arundel of Canterbury made a list of 55 reasons why I was undeserving and read them out to them, that sanctimonious scheming snake-in-the grass. If I'd actually given up the throne, you know, like they said I had, then I don't think he would have needed to slag me off like that, would he? Then Henry dressed up like a king and had a coronation, and he was in.'

'And then you didn't have long left.'

'Me and many others, my friend, me and many, many others.'

'King Richard, I'm really, really grateful to you for telling me all this. It must be hard for you.'

'You are mortal man, I am beyond worldly care, in a better place, Anna by my side. It's not too bad.' Damian was ready to leave but there was something else to do. Something emotional. He tensed himself, braced himself and went through with it.

'King Richard, I had a dream about you.'

'I felt it.'

'There was someone else there. Do you know who she was?'

'Yes, I know her. After all the killing the first time, when things had settled and I got the throne back from them, we became friends.' Damian wanted to ask 'lovers?' but felt that was an unworthy question. He didn't want to go too far and let his curiosity spoil a meaningful relationship with the dead king.

'Friends?'

'Yes, we were friends.'

'Do you think you could tell me who she was?'

'No, I'm sorry, she doesn't want you to know, but you already know anyway.' Tantalising impasse. That seemed to be the last word. Damian's envelopes had not been detailed enough for this Romana Clay sub-enquiry and he needed to get back home, get back on the internet and look for her. Anyway, Romana wasn't her real name. It never had been. He'd just made it up.

'Thank you King Richard.'

'Thank you, and thank you for not waking Anna. Thank you. You're doing a great job.' Damian smiled. The compliment pleased him. He made a stiff and courteous bow towards the king and queen, turned and made his way out.

36

Teasing through the evidence he'd obtained and thinking out how he would use it to construct his enquiry had been easy on the train, but was not conducive to problem-free motoring and he'd absent-mindedly missed two motorway junctions, had to doomak his way back to the right road, and was now nearing home.

'Braggadocio'. That was a mouthful. Delicious. Crunchy, like a mixed salad. Was he a braggart? He wanted to brag to Lorna Dune and Harry-Dan Dolmetscher and send them a bragging email but didn't want to seem too much of a show-off.

The day-out to Lincoln and York had turned into a pretty manic 72-hour operation. Did you have to be manic and single-minded to get things done? It was an unsettling thought. He tidied it away into a box for troublesome ideas which he kept out-of-sight on top of his mind-wardrobe, and concentrated on his driving. He didn't want anything to prevent him concretising his ideas, like an accident, especially one his fault due to inattentive carelessness.

He bragged to Harry-Dan as soon as he could, as intended, about how well he was doing and the reply, though coming quickly, still lacked, Damian believed, something of the earlier warmth they'd shared, but he had asked to see the final draft, so Damian was reassured and knew it was all up to him not to let Harry-Dan down. And he wouldn't.

Damian had four whole days to craft his diatribe against

Henry IV. Plenty of time but there was a theoretical, maybe existential, stumbling block to overcome; he would have to write it up using the same old history nonsense: guessing what people were thinking at such and such a time, making weak inferences, conjecturising, stretching points, bending things to make them fit the…, the narr…, to fit the narra…, to fit the narrative. There would be a narrative. But would that be the truth? Could a narrative ever be true, the truth?

Each morning he came out of his corner of the ring, saluted his opponent and wrestled with them all day and into the evening. Friendly, chaste and winsome spirits visited with suggestions and solutions in the night, for which he was grateful the next day. Damian wanted to look beyond words, words like reflections on windows looking back at you, to the wordless truths beyond and explore this…, this…, other dimension, the human side. Was that pathos? Was it about pitying them? Were they pathetic? They had been dead too long to be pitied really. Was it empathy? No way, he didn't want to be them, it had been hard enough wearing ballet shoes in York; the woman with the Wellbeing-You! T-shirt had liked wearing them and he'd hated it; where was the empathy in that?

Sympathy? He did sympathise with them. History's grind-stone had taken their everything and turned it to dust. Even if they were dust, sunbeam motes in an otherwise gloomy church, if History had double-crossed them, wasn't there an obligation on him to tell it right? Grave-robbing academics went on painstaking excavations to find pottery, beads and arrow-heads to find a story. Usually they didn't find one; there was an infinite number of archive-boxes filled with bones, shards and fragments somewhere. He was doing the same thing as them, except that his site had already been dug over. He would reinterpret, go to museum basements for forgotten artefacts and tell a different story to the one laid down in history as fact.

If Damian's intellectualising got too much he could nip out on his new upgraded and over-accessorised scooter which went like an absolute bomb, nailed to the road by top-quality Italian shock-absorbers, and blast around till his head cleared. He felt more sympathetic. He was sympatico. almost narkless with dawdling motorists and would try to make small-talk in shops. getting generally more genial the closer he came to completion, until he reached the apogee; his 5000 words were done and he just needed to let Harry-Dan have the once over before the deadline, as promised.

Dolmetcher's reply email was full of praise, starting with:

'Damian, you are an absolute legend. You've nailed it in the nick of time you old sluggard.'

Damian nodded in approval at the double-edged compliment, read the rest of the short laudatory text, smugged up his face and opened the 'Read me' attachment which made him smile; a sort of heraldry design in the middle of the screen with 'Kleio' on it, out of which hatched an animated yellow smiley-face which grew bigger, developed arms with thumbs up on the end, bounced around, started to sweat, opened and closed its mouth, and flopped out a big red tongue which flapped about and then it all exploded into yellow blobs all over the screen.

Damian laughed out loud. There was just enough time to indulge in a little deferred gratification for old time's sake so he held off uploading his submission to the host website platform and imagined Lorna's happy face when she read his stuff, it was new and was classy, maybe she would get some benefit off the back of it, like a promotion. He made himself a mug of tea, had a look in the paper to relax and get in the zone before initiating the triumphal sequence.

Doomak made its presence felt in waves. The computer wouldn't switch back on. It did this from time to time. Damian didn't mind this mechanical idiosyncrasy and was used to dealing with it. Something was sticky with the switch and he had special ways of pressing it and one of them worked.

'Good old doomak, never say die.'

Damian was careless with his tea and nearly knocked the slops of his mug over the keyboard.

'Doomak, methinks thou triest too hard.'

He got the website up, entered his details and began the submission process. The machine wanted to know which program he wanted to use to open the EPQ file with. Each time he tried a row of squares, symbols and letters appeared.

This nonsense had happened a lot over the years as his technology got outdated and the world moved on but it hadn't done that for a while. This wasn't the time for that. Damian racked his brains but his reserves of technological know-how, already depleted, were quickly spent as was the oxygen-level in the room, or so it seemed. Dread put a chilling heat on his face and dried his mouth. Fear tightened his chest and trembled his fingers as they tried to tap their way to safety. Damian was buried in numbing nausea. Nothing would work. He had a back-up on a memory stick, it's icon showed on the screen; a message said that the Gaunt file couldn't be opened because it wasn't in the correct location. But he could see it. The machine wouldn't let him do something he'd done a thousand times before. And the website was jammed and wouldn't let him write anything explaining the situation.

Hopelessly, the window of opportunity slowly closed. Then it was shut, the deadline passed. He folded up the laptop, brought it to his chest cradling it in his arms, letting his head fall forward, beaten, closed his eyes and wished that he was crying. That would have been the right thing to do. Anybody would have sympathised with him if he had, he was sure.

Beaten by doomak, yes, but Damian wouldn't give it any more satisfaction. He'd done a good job and enjoyed doing it. It hadn't needed any supervision by Harry-Dan Dolmetscher or Lorna Dune or anyone else. It was his and he'd done it alone. It could be written out from memory, in a slightly different way maybe, and sent to Lorna with a covering letter explaining things and apologising.

He put the laptop aside, forgave it, and wanted to go outside to get some fresh air. His coat was in an alcove by the front door where he kept the vacuum-cleaner and he'd put it on and was opening the door when he noticed a memento of his mother on a shelf – a large black-and-white framed photograph. He took it out and searched it with his eyes. She was sat down, on a hillside somewhere, looking over her shoulder at the photographer, with a playful, haughty and enigmatic 'what are you doing here?' expression on her face. His dad had taken the picture, taken it by surprise, developed it himself, probably cropped it to get the head and shoulders full-frame and enlarged it. A moment in time. The photograph was a fact, but what she meant by her look could now never be known. Tears came to his eyes. That was worth crying about. He closed the door.

Damian gave himself a lie-in the next day and wasn't around when the dawn came to see if he wanted to go out and play again. He missed her but there would be other times. The move-on schedule would be bacon roll, coffee, papers till... about eleven. Then what? Scooter ride? Why not? Damian packed some books and magazines that needed catching up with, and went off, moving on. His sabbatical had been successful but now he was free and could get back to the daily grind of doing what he liked, but watching the pennies, not getting carried away.

He scootered to a castle but didn't go in, preferring to imagine the medieval comings and goings from a distance, cheaply. Later, he found an attractive riverside location near an abbey and loafed there like a pro. The weather may have been warm but Damian knew he came over cool with his sweet scooter. It wasn't his fault he looked that way; he was just an ordinary guy out to enjoy himself in an ordinary way and if that was cool, then so be it. Lengthening shadows moved to shift him and he headed back home, getting some tweet and booze on the way, ready for a decent evening watching something: maybe a DVD, or some comedy.

37

His fab new scooter was up on its centre-stand, secured to a post with a heavy chain through its back-wheel and he was just about to flip the seat up and take out the rain-cover from the storage space beneath when a familiar voice made him turn round; the driver's door of a car parked nearby was open and disgorging Harry-Dan Dolmetscher himself.

'I'm very glad to see you indeed. I wasn't sure when you were coming back, or would at all, so I'm bloody glad to see that you have. Are you ready, or nearly? I hung on for you. You look ready.'

'Harry-Dan! Hi,' bumbled Damian, 'yes, I'm...,'

'That's great, we can go just like you are, no need to change, you look fine.'

'Yes but..., I've got this...,' Damian waved at his shopping strapped to the rear chrome rack with stretchy bungees. Damian was never at his best when caught off-guard. He could think on his feet but not in the way that means instantly taking in a situation, giving a witty comeback and gaining the upper hand no matter what. He was a cogitator and being surprised usually meant saying the wrong thing and having to make amends. Harry-Dan dismissed his reservations.

'Bring it with you, we've just got enough time, I'll carry it if you like,' and he started undoing the fastenings, put them inside the bag containing Damian's shopping and stuff and hoisted it onto his shoulder in a fumbling blur.

'Harry-Dan, it's...,'

'I know Damian, let's get going and I'll fill you in.' Damian was befuddled by all this flurrying and a bit annoyed. It was almost doomaky, but he'd had a good day out, just got back and was glad to see his interlocutor – he would be able to tell him all about the woes of last night face to face. Damian started to speak but H-D's purposeful stride was a notch more powerful and purposeful than Damian's and it was hard to keep up with him. Hard to keep up and speak at the same time without garbling a bit out of breath.

Harry-Dan was sometimes speaking as well, making an intertwined double-helix of confused dialogue, but Damian was able to pick up that they were going to his local favourite pub again, which he didn't mind as he'd had a good day out and a pub evening would be a good finisher, especially with Harry-Dan Dolmetscher, who certainly appreciated them too, and knew what they were for.

The pacey scurrying got Damian hot and red-faced as he struggled to take his armoured jacket off: unzipping it, pulling his arm out, then the other, then folding it into a bundle over his helmet, all without stopping. Heavy but cool-looking denim armoured trousers, a bit too big, further encumbered and impeded progress. By the time they got to the pub, Damian was pooped and glad they'd got there. That wasn't the end of it. Harry-Dan strode on, past a pleadingly vacant table that would have been ideal, to the entrance.

'Shall we have a smoke Harry-Dan, out here?' gasped Damian in the momentary pause at the door.

'No time,' was the reply, although Damian couldn't really hear it as Harry-Dan said it to no one in particular, in quite a low voice, almost a mumble, as he was ushering Damian through.

Inside, Harry-Dan shouted something over the heads of the crowd of customers at the bar and carried on steering Damian through the throng and round the corner to a point where the bar-flap had been raised, through it and round the back. Damian brimmed with queries but their pace was relentless and didn't let him get a word out. A turn to the left, a narrow corridor, a non-bar area with boxes of crisps and sundry stock, a cream-coloured off-white door, up some stairs with a brown carpet which might once have been colourful and patterned, a turn to the left onto a little landing, a few more steps up and they were in a long narrow, crowded room: dimly lit, lined with framed photographs of jazz musicians, with a low stage at the far end, under lights.

Harry-Dan took Damian's helmet and jacket and dropped them, along with the shopping bag, under a table and rested against the short bar at the end of the room opposite the stage.

The room was hot, loud, and packed with people grouped around bar tables nattering to each other excitedly and Dolmetscher had to shout to be heard.

'Damian, do you want a drink?' Damian signalled affirmation by nodding six times in quick succession, too knackered to do more. He was dripping and out of breath. The beer, when it came, was not there for long. Opening his mouth created a powerful vacuum and suction emptied the glass in a fast double-swig. It was his favourite beer. Dolmetscher got another and he took in the scene as he tried to recover composure. It was obviously an upstairs music venue and tonight looked like being a sell-out.

'Harry-Dan...,' it was time for explanations and Damian was

ready to get one or give one. He didn't like being surprised but he did like surprises, and it looked like there was going to be some quality entertainment tonight and sundry good times were, he sensed, in the offing. Dolmetscher shouted over the hubbub again.

'Damian, so sorry, there was no time. It's nearly time. Make sure you see me back here tomorrow at eleven. Shall I write it down? Eleven.' Damian nodded.

'Yeah, ok, eleven,' it was loud. He had to exaggerate the words to be heard.

'It's nearly time, at the end, make sure you say "I autodidact".'

'I what?' It was so loud in there.

'AYE – AWE – TOE – DIE – DACT.'

'What?'

'AYE – AWE – TOE – DIE – DACT. Say it back to me!'

'AYE. AWE. TOE. DIE. DACT.' Damian was oblivious and rightly didn't know what the other was talking about.

'Right, now's the time, take it with you.' Harry-Dan nudged, shoved, and swayed Damian, drink in hand, down through the centre-aisle, past the noisily chatting groups and onto the stage, under the lights. Damian was nonplussed. Harry-Dan pushed a button on the P.A. stack to turn on the microphone, showily tapped it twice to get attention, and spoke.

'Good evening all and thanks for coming to one of our regular regional get-togethers. First time here but I'm sure it won't be our last.'

Damian was at the side of the stage about six feet away.

'Tonight's entertainment is a diatribe against Henry IV by Damian Email. Diatribe, a forceful and bitter attack,' Harry-

Dan pulled some faces at the audience, making them laugh, working the room, 'but bitter is as bitter does so I won't sugar the pill any longer, please give him a warm welcome.'

Rowdy pub applause followed with a couple of whistles and a dash of yeahs. Harry-Dan swayed Damian to centre-stage by the mic stand and sashayed away to a table in the front at the side.

Damian had been taken by surprise again. He had a drink in his hand. The lights were on him. Immobile in a tonic way, he stopped time and saw rabbits in headlights forgetting their lines at a public poetry recital. Were other clichés available? He could lick his lips, stammer a bit, wipe his forehead with his hand, blink. He had a drink.

He was the centre of attention, they were expectant, animated and joyful but if he showed fear they would despise him, his fear would chill their hearts. They would sympathise with his suffering and hate him for it, because that's not what they were there for.

Damian finished his drink. The silence was not quite embarrassing yet. Sat next to Harry-Dan was Lorna. He could put on a show of recognising her, he could reel in shock, really milk it, but he'd run out of clichés and finally got it; he was on stage in an upstairs club and he was the entertainment. They had come to hear his diatribe and watch him do it. Well so bloody well be it.

Damian grubbed around for a handy and suitable latinism to wake himself out of his trance, found 'alea jacta est': the die is cast, and used it for his opening line.

'Alea jacta est.'

38

The start was a little uncertain but his systematic layering of arguments, backed up with well-made points soon won his audience over and they were right behind him, savouring every rhetorical device, relishing his subtle accentuating and clever pausing which were never arch or clumsy.

Damian was one-step ahead of what he was saying, like a maestro-musician playing himself like a fiddle, puppeteering his own puppet-self. Henry IV was going down and wouldn't be able to get back up from the mat for a long time, maybe never. There was no coming back from this diatribe. Damian slowed time down and a tonic immobility inversion let him dance around in it, so that what felt an age to him was a mere twenty-five minutes to the on-lookers.

When he'd wrapped up the overwhelming evidence into a convincing conclusion, throwing in a couple of last-minute ad hominem jabs to the solar plexus, he rematerialized back into his own shoes on the stage where he'd started, said his damning end-piece and looked back at the audience, waiting for the acclamation that was rightly his.

There was an embarrassed oppressive silence. A cough. Something was wrong. The lights were hot. He couldn't see them. His throat dried, a familiar black bile of terror seeped from vital organs in his guts, panic enzymes began dripping from ducts, his skin went clammy, his tongue swollen-up in a dry mouth. Time had slowed again but in a really bad way.

He hadn't properly reincorporated himself from the

inverted tonic mobility paradigm; the materialisation coordinates were fluxed and he was being badly retrograded. Something was moving around in the corner. A person. Moving strangely. Almost inhuman. A gambolling jackanapes. It kept opening and closing its mouth like a bizarre gaping fish-face-man and was pointing at itself and making big exaggerated arm movements to do it. Fish-face-man. Pointing at himself, Fish-man, you shouldn't be pointing at yourself. Fish-man, you should be pointing at your eye. It should be your eye. Why? He remembered.

'I..., I autodidact.' The audience rose to their feet as if he'd just finished the best thing they'd ever seen and deserved an immediate standing ovation, then and there. Now.

'EEE! EEE! AYE!' they cheered in unison as they pushed forward to the stage area.

'EEE! EEE! AYE!' they cheered again, louder still, as they came towards him, some clumsily stepping over awkwardly placed chairs and tables, eager to be nearer.

'EEE! EEE! AYE!' roaring now and they'd nearly all made it to the stage area. Damian hadn't properly come round and was still dozy but the crowd put smelling salts under his nose and woke him up with their next three colossal shouts, each more definite and conclusive than the one before.

'AYE!' They raised their glasses in a toast, and lowered them.

'AYE!' They raised their glasses in a toast, and lowered them.

'**AYE**!' and thirty or so glasses were raised but this time they didn't stop to salute but kept going in the vigorous and energetic motion of a full sloshing throw to chuck their contents straight at Damian, mostly hitting him in the face, soaking him, as if the very air around him had liquefied at the flick of a switch. He was pulled off the dais and surrounded by a kaleidoscope of congratulatory faces swaying around him, all talking and smiling at the same time. Damian smiled back, bemused, excited, as he was pawed and pummelled. He'd done it. They were delighted. He'd done it! It was strange, bizarre, intoxicating and they were deliriously ecstaticly delighted with him. They'd loved it, he'd done it, and they'd soaked him for it. Wow! Wow! Amazing! Amazing!

Harry-Dan pushed through to Damian, grabbed his hand and shook it heartily, pumping it mightily, then, without letting go, Harry-Dan turned and spoke to the pressing people around them, raising their joined hands up like a boxing referee announcing the winner. Damian couldn't hear what he said for the noise and the next thing he was being manoeuvred through the collage of grinning faces, hands offered and shaken, claps on the back, some hugs, towards the bar at the back and to a table where a pint of Damian's favourite beer was waiting for him. Slipstreaming just behind came Lorna with some others and they all plonked themselves breathlessly down at it together.

Damian didn't have time to think. Astonishment was the new normal and people were talking to him from the left, from the right, and from the front, beaming at him directly, all jabbering at once. Even his hair was getting a ruffling from well-wishers. It was several orders of magnitude more intense than his wedding disco had been, and that had been pretty wild. Lorna was talking to people coming up to her, nodding her head and showing a lovely wide and generous smile, and was maybe explaining things with her good-looking hands, making shapes with them and moving her fingers around. Lorna introduced another woman who looked a bit like her. Over the din, someone told him it was her sister Claire and she was wearing an 'Anxietyup-Yours!' tee-shirt which really attracted his attention, and double-denim, like her sister. It was all much too much but he was liking it a lot.

There was a buffet and somebody brought over a selection of tweet for the table. Little chicken and tarragon sandwiches, sausage rolls and scotch eggs, all authentic and delicious and served with various relishes. Damian corrected himself, Claire and Lorna weren't actually in double-denim, that's all denim, they were in denim, cheesecloth and denim sandwiches but double-denim sounded better. Trays of chips were there, fried eggs on heated plates and ham too. They all tucked in and it went on like that: beery, convivial, jovial, wonderful until Damian, escaping Earth's gravity, was put into a deep-space sleep for the interstellar trip and no more could be remembered.

39

It should have been anticlimactic when Damian woke up but it had been such an amazing night that there was no need to come down, and it was nice to put the jigsaw puzzle of recollections back together.

His head was not too bad and he was up early showing what a Spartan he was. Maybe the hangover would be one of those late developing ones, or maybe not, it might kick in any time, so what? A small price to pay. OK, some preventative pills just in case. He'd got back, not sure how, all his stuff was there, nothing missing, some of it smelling of wine and beer and he had a beer mat with Clare's name, he noted its correct spelling, and number on it, along with 'Call me', and 'See you at eleven!' in different hand-writing. Damian was aware that a little smile was playing at the corners of his mouth which the ignorant could have called a smirk but he knew it wasn't.

He felt pretty fine, cooked a good breakfast, bagged up his booze-soaked clothes, did some other routine stuff to kill a bit of time and walked back to the pub, rather than scootering there, as he wanted a bit of exercise and fresh air and, in any case, he might've been over the limit. Damian knew that Harry-Dan would be inside at a corner table drinking coffee as the bar was being spruced up ready for the day so he went straight inside and was surprised not to see him already there. Maybe he was upstairs cleaning up. He'd ask the lady behind the bar.

'We don't have an upstairs venue like that,' replied the

woman, getting shirty at being asked the same question three times in different ways by the persistent stranger. Damian was raising his voice, getting agitated and feeling toxifying adrenalinous poisons erupt from their glands. The bar-lady was getting agitated as well, looking over his shoulder and waving her hand around. Mystified and queasy, Damian turned and could see Harry-Dan, partially screened by a partition, silently chortling and guffawing his head off and then unblocking a suppressed hysterical fit of unrestrained mirth at full volume.

H-D let it all out and his exhibition filled the room. He came stumbling over but still couldn't stop himself laughing and wheezing, sobbing for breath, clapping his knees, doubling over sometimes and pulling faces. He was having a right-royal laughter attack and should have been dressed as a clown.

'I'm sorry. I'm sorry,' he gasped between laugh-sobs, 'I can't resist it. I just can't resist it. I can never resist it. Thanks Barbara, great job.' His face florid and tearful, he now looked gleefully miserable.

'Oh…, Oh…,' wiping his eyes with his fingers, 'Oh…, I owe you Barbara. I owe you big time. Oh man, that was a damn good one.' The spate was abating and Harry-Dan was getting a grip on himself. 'Come over here. let's sit down. Man oh man oh man oh man!'

Damian was getting tired of Harry-Dan's appreciation of his own one-sided prank. Deep-breathing and sighs calmed things down until Harry-Dan was able to fill Damian in with what had been going on last night and it had gone very well indeed. It had been a 'viva voce', an oral examination so to speak, and Damian had been accepted into the order by all the members and it had been unambiguously unanimous. Damian had to get Harry-Dan to be more explicit; he was short-changing him on detail which Harry Dan admitted and apologised for.

The regional 'Kleio' chapter of the Autodidactiiae had met and accepted him as a brother. He had been scrutinised, proved himself worthy and he'd been taken in. Dolmetscher explained how it was done, how acolytes had to make, what they called 'progress' but it wasn't the normal kind of progress, it was more like a 'stately progress' or a 'royal progress' or a 'pilgrim's progress'. It was progressing along a path, not necessarily progressing as in 'getting better' and that path couldn't, mustn't be an easy one. It wasn't allowed to be easy. Sometimes it had to be made rocky and stony. The path had to be difficult otherwise you couldn't progress along it properly and you couldn't get in to the Autodidactiiae unless you could show that you could.

'Damian, I have to…, I must apologise to you.'

'No need Harry-Dan.' Damian was still perplexed, 'There's no need. It was a funny joke.'

'No, it's not about that, it's about this.' and he took off his necklace pendant thing that Damian had thought was the Phial of Galadriel and placed it over Damian's head, saying:

'This is the phial with the philtre.' Damian wasn't really a necklace-pendant person.

'Do I have to wear it all the time?'

'Not at all. I just have to put it on you once. You can get all different types. Look what this one does.' H-D leant forward, grasped the pendant and pulled the end off with his other hand. It was a USB stick.

'It's the antidote.' If there was a curve, Damian was behind it.

'To what?'

'To the virus I put in your laptop, you'll be able to get it all back.'

'You...,You...,' Harry-Dan butted back before the inevitable torrent of abuse broke out.

'Listen Damian, please...,' Damian was still reaching for his pistol.

'This wasn't a joke on you. This was a therapeutic intervention, wisely suggested by Lorna, and executed by myself, which had as its object your unblocking.'

'My unblocking? But...,'

'Yes, writing down your enquiry could not effect the necessary changes to your sub-conscious which were needed to bring about your historical wellbeing. You would, at a primitive level, have felt compromised. We had to take it away from you, to de-exteriorise it, so that it came from the heart. Your heart. Your experience. A tale told at the end of a journey.'

'Well, Mr Harry-Dan Dolmetscher, thanks, I had a great time last night, and today was funny too. You nearly had me.' Damian put the safety-catch back on and holstered it.

'Thanks Mr Damian Email, I did too. Between ourselves, I worry that I enjoy the next day too much. My joke always works and I never get sick of it. I do it over and over again.' Damian knew what he meant.

'So Damian, that's it for now. You'll get everything you need off the stick and more. I've got business in town.'

Damian didn't want the moment to end. He wanted to extend it as its savouring couldn't be deferred.

'What about the Autodidactiiae, who else is one?'

'You get to be able to tell other ones. You develop a sixth sense.'

'Is Lorna one?'

'Duh-uh!'

'Is she?'

'Of course she is.'

'Is her sister one?'

'She was there, wasn't she?'

'So is she?'

'Of course she is.' The new inductees often came over as dim but he, an experienced practitioner, was forgiving of their callow lack of insight.

'Damian you're doing my head in. I suppose you must be in shock or something.'

'What about...,' and Damian went through the well-known historians who'd been on the list at the start: McGrayth, Landscape, blah and blah. Only the rude irritating one wasn't one, he'd gone pedanticly rogue and been booted out recently. Apart from him, they all were ones. It was a broad church and he shouldn't over-focus on prominence, was the advice.

It was more about brotherly and sisterly love of history in the Kleio chapter. All were as equals in the order and that, yes, it did take one to know one and Damian agreed that, yes, he'd thought they probably were one before he'd asked; he'd been playing dumb for a joke and no, he wasn't surprised about Pinchman's fall from grace.

Harry-Dan and Damian went halves on the modest bill and parted as brothers, brother autodidactiiaes.

40

It had all been most satisfactory and he'd been much lauded for his perspicacity, or was it perspicaceouness. He hadn't needed the plaudits but it was extremely agreeable to have been so celebrated the night before like that; he'd been accepted into the fraternity-sorority, and was now one of them, without even knowing it.

If that wasn't deserving then what was, he'd like to know. A sense of perspective would have to be kept, it mustn't go to his head. Still, it made a big change from the normal run of things; the normal run of things was that you showed someone something you'd put your soul into and they started stirring up your humours, mixing them up in your bowels by telling you what they thought of it, trying to be helpful and constructive, suggesting how you could make it even better, but actually strangling you with poisonous doomak.

That hadn't been last night at all, he thought, walking back, it had all gone one way, but it didn't feel quite over, there was something left to do and by the time he'd returned to Epsilon Precinct he'd made up his mind to go and see her, on the scooter, and make a trip of it, right then, right now, and half an hour later he was sound-tracking his blat up the motorway with:

Head out on the highway
>   tuh tuh-tuh tuh tuh tuh tuh-tuh-tuh-tuh
Looking for adventure
>   tuh tuh tuh-tuh-tuh-tuh-tuh, tuh tuh tuh...

Motorways were brutally efficient at slicing their way
through the country and the riding was always dull, although
the weather this time was perfect: golden sunshine like in
California but a lot greener, with a permanent heat-haze on
the horizon of the hot tarmac. There was nothing else to do
but think and keep a constant tempo, 70 mph. Damian's head
was almost devoid of post-booze thrubbing but the experience
of the night before had been profoundly psychadeliceous and
bits of it broke the surface of his consciousness as he drove
along: Harry-Dan on fire taking him round the room to meet
everyone, a blur, a chat with Lorna, a blur, a long chat with her
sister, a blur, but not so much. Less of one.

They had been talking about last names. She'd returned from
America and gone back to 'Dunny', her maiden name, because
she didn't mind it, but there, in America, she'd been..., what was
it? She'd been ..., 'Pork'? No. Like pork. No, it was actually
Pork. No, it wasn't. It was actually 'Hogsflesh'. She'd been
Hogsflesh in America. It came back to him now. She'd been
Hogsflesh there but it hadn't worked out and now she was Ms
Dunny. Claire Dunny. No, it wasn't. It was Clare Dunny. Get
it right.

He recalled talking to her about names, words, origins and
etymologies. She hadn't been bored. She'd been agog, with a
lot to say for herself. It was indistinct in places but bits stuck
out clearly, like her tee-shirt with 'Anxietyup-Yours!' on. That
was a bit punky. Might actually be offensive. Clare Dunny, a bit
like her sister but different. Sexier. Lorna was sexy, but Clare
was sexier, and single.

A temporary road sign marked the edge of Hoveringham;
a large salmon-pink metal panel with a big thumbs-up graphic

in white and the letters A.C.E above. It had been some time since Damian had seen one of these and they'd become a rarity. So rare that there was a collectable after-market for old ones and they were more often seen being used as ironic decorative pieces in bars and funky modern eating-places, than on the road like this one. Damian raised a mental eyebrow and headed to his destination.

If he hadn't mixed up Hoveringham in Nottinghamshire with somewhere similar-sounding in Essex, maybe Havering, then he could have come before on his way to Lincoln, but he hadn't got it all straightened out then. He parked by the lych-gate and went straight to the church. On the door inside its porch was a 3-inch square salmon-pink A.C.E sticker with the same logo. Damian could read 'Wellbeing-You!' in tiny print at the bottom and there was an uplifting, calming and reassuring message.

'Well done Rick, you're getting to be ubiquitous', thought Damian. The door into the church was locked. This was a bit like those pandemic days when things were closed like this. A.C.E meant Active Contact Enquiry. They were very good at it now and often you never noticed you were in one. Whoever opened it up must be part of the A.C.E and were quarantining. What were those people who opened up churches called? Sacristans? Sextons? Church wardens? Damian was philosophical about being thwarted and nurdled the early Fleetwood Mac 'Oh well' riff in his musical mind's eye:

> 'Duh durdle durdle da durdle da-da-da
> > duh durdle durdle da da da da duh duh duh.
> Duh durdle durdle da durdle da-da-da
> > duh durdle durdle da da da da duh duh duh.'

'Oh well.'

That's how it went. Oh well, so what? He could come back again. The pleasure had been deferred for him, by circumstances. He liked that.

'Churchyards like this, on days like these, after shady bowers by cool streams of course, are the places of utmost and finest repose,' said Damian to himself, as he leant against the sunny stonework of the church, and imagined himself filling a long-stemmed pipe with the finest Virginia, like Gandalf.

You could look around at all the buildings nearby and know for sure that whatever place in time they came from, this place, this church, had been here the longest. It put you at the very centre of things. Ok, it was ever so slightly disappointing not to be able to go in to accost Elizabeth Fitzalan's effigy with:

'You are the lady in red and I claim my five pounds,' but oh well, so what?

Elizabeth had been married to Thomas Mowbray, Henry's one-time partner and was mother of another Thomas Mowbray, who'd been executed with Archbishop Scrope. Her father was the sly and devious Richard Fitzalan, the executed 4th earl of Arundel no less. Issued from that Arundel brood of vipers, she'd married a hood turned good and mothered a rebel without a future. Married 5 times she lay gisant in the church next to her third husband who, most peculiarly, was one of the few soldiers in history to have been murdered in battle, and not killed normaly.

The Haxey Hood legend said that it was the wife of a John Mowbray who lost her cloak that windy day in the fourteenth century. Mowbrays were basically always Thomas or John. She was mother of a John but not married to one; she'd married a Thomas. Damian looked at her picture on the envelope. Her effigy wore a well-sculpted cloak that certainly looked light enough to billow out behind her as she went around on horseback, if it was windy or she was galloping quickly. You could even imagine it caught by a sudden squall and blowing right off her, if it had come, somehow, unclasped. Strange how the authentic and folkloric legend behind the game hadn't retained the name of the fine lady who'd come undone that day. Evidence of patriarchal dominance perhaps?

Damian knew that it was Elizabeth Fitzalan who had put herself in his vision of dead King Richard to point him in the right direction, towards the supine tomb sculptures, so that he would be able to find a truth so powerful that Henry's reputation would shatter, hammered by on the anvil of history, by he, 'Vulcan' Email. Damian knew that the Haxey Hood lady was also Elizabeth Fitzalan but he would keep that to himself. 'Who was he, Damian Email?' he silently proclaimed, 'to argue with the legend. Print the legend!' Let it be the unknown wife of a certain indeterminate John Mowbray, and not Elizabeth Mowbray, née Fitzalan then. She wouldn't mind. She'd done her job and so had he. He'd come back for her.

The stones around him were warmed by the sun and radiated their heat energy back out into his back and hands. This must be what they call 'basking'. He was basking in it, lapping it up. He felt well, being him.

'Well', was that from 'wealth', as in the 'common wealth'? Had it used to be 'weal-ath', sort of Saxon, Chaucerian maybe? Was 'whole' the same word? Was 'heal-ath' the same word as 'weal-ath' back then? You needed the right words for the right things. Words were old things.

Damian took the beer-mat from his pocket and looked at the number written on it. A little non-smirking smile curved the corner of his mouth as the prospect of principled and deferred gratification delighted. It was so warm there, at the centre of things. Damian closed his eyes, the better to be fully aware of the soomak in the moment. Breathed in. Breathed out. Why put it off? He got his phone from the car and texted Clare: 'Well?' and it rang back straightaway.

Epilogue

It's Terpsichore's regular beach volleyball session on Mount Parnassus and it's four against four, but she's sitting this one out and trying to find the best musical accompaniment for the other winsome female-formed players wearing flattering garments.

She experiments with little finger cymbals, a tambourine, pan pipes, a lyre. She hasn't quite got it yet but it's coming and it's nice to have a break from dancing. Kleio is a bit heavy-footed but getting better and quite competitive. Now all the muses can have a break if they want one.

Dramatis Personae

1 | **Elizabeth of Lancaster 1364-1426** St Mary's Church, Burford, Worcestershire. Wife of John Holland 1352-1400, 1st Duke of Exeter, 1st Earl of Huntingdon.

2 | **Katherine Swynford 1350-1403** Lincoln Cathedral. Long-term lover of John of Gaunt and last wife. Entombed with her daughter and Joan Beaufort 1379-1440.

3 | **Richard Scrope 1350-1405** York Minster. Archbishop of York 1398-1405.

4 | **Sir Thomas Erpingham 1355-1428** Norwich Cathedral and Erpingham Gate, Norwich.

5 | **The Black Prince 1330-1376** Canterbury Cathedral Heir to the throne. Father of Richard II.

6 | **Henry IV 1367-1413** Canterbury Cathedral. AKA Henry Bolingbroke, Earl of; Derby, Northampton, Hereford. Duke of; Hereford, Lancaster, and Joan of Navarre 1368-1437.

7 | **Richard Fitzalan 1306-1376** Chichester Cathedral 3rd Earl of Arundel and **Eleanor of Lancaster 1318-1372.**

8 | **Richard II 1367-1400** Westminster Abbey King of England and **Anne of Bohemia 1366-1394.**

9 | **Elizabeth Fitzalan 1366-1425** St Michael's Church. Hoveringham, Nottinghamshire.
    Wife of Thomas Mowbray, Earl of Nottingham, 1st Duke of Norfolk 1366-1399 (their marriage 1384-1399), and Sir Robert Goushill 1362-1403.

Extras, with effigies

Ralph Neville 1364-1425 St Mary's Church, Staindrop, County Durham. 1st Earl of Northumberland and to his right, effigy only: **Joan Beaufort 1379-1440**, daughter of John of Gaunt and Katherine Swynford, 14 children, being the grandmother of Edward IV and Richard III and to his left, effigy only: **Margaret Stafford 1364-1396**, 6 children

Edward 111, 1312-1377. Westminster Abbey, and **Phillipa of Hainault 1313-1369**.

Henry Despenser, 1341-1406. Norwich Cathedral. Archbishop of York. Carving on misericorde.

Sir John Beauchamp of Holt, 1344-1388. Worcester cathedral and **Joan Fitzwith**. Possible misattribution.

Eleanor de Bohun, 1366-1399. Westminster Abbey Wife of Thomas of Woodstock 1355-97, 1st Duke of Gloucester, youngest son of Edward III and leader of the Lords Appellant.

Phillipa de Mohun, 1367-1431. Westminster Abbey. 3rd wife of Edward of Norwich aka 2nd Duke of York (marriage 1398-1415), son of Edmund of Langley.

Thomas Fitzalan, 1381-1415. Arundel Chapel, Arundel Castle. 5th Earl of Arundel and **Beatrice of Portugal 1380-1439**. Married 1405.

Sir Bernard Brocas senior, 1330-1395. Westminster Abbey.

Edmund of Langley, 1341-1402. All Saints' Church. Kings Langley, Hertfordshire. 1st Duke of York, 4th son of Edward III. Satuette also on Edward III's tomb in Westminster Abbey.

Margaret Ferrers, ?-1406 Brass. St Mary's Church. Warwick. Wife of Thomas de Beauchamp, 12th Earl of Warwick.

Henry V, 1386-1422. Westminster Abbey, effigy head from 1971 and, seperately, **Catherine de Valois 1401-1437**, married 1420.

I, Autodidact: Soundtrack

1   633 Squadron - *Ron Goodwin*

2   I'm on my way - *Dean Parrish*

3   Baby, you've got it - *The Action*

4   The great gig in the sky - *Pink Floyd*

5   Therapy - *M*

6   Don't burst my bubble - *Small Faces*

7   I'm free - *The Soupdragons*

8   Look what the wind blew in - *Thin Lizzy*

9   Go! - *Public Service Broadcasting*

10 Swords of a thousand men - *Tenpole Tudor*

11 Cry Baby - *Janis Joplin*

12 Ride my see saw - *The Moody Blues*

13 Man with a harmonica - *Ennio Morricone*

14 May it be - *Enya*

15 I'm alive - *Don Fardon*

16 Savoy Truffle - *The Beatles*

17 Searching - *Roy Ayers*

18 Song for the Siren - *The Cocteau Twins*

19 Private Investigation - *Dire Straits*

20 Should I stay or should I go - *The Clash*

21 Stop your sobbing - *The Kinks*

22 The killing moon - *Echo and the Bunnymen*

23 The gambler - *Kenny Rogers*

24 You can get it if you really want it - *Jimmy Cliff*

Acknowledgements

Wikkipedia, ad infinitum.

Advice and contributions from G Watson, J-M Jot, C Garratt, S Wilson

Artwork contributions from B Bluett and M Van Dalen

Particular thanks to L Johnston.

Translation of Richard II's tomb inscription.
https://www.westminster-abbey.org/abbey-commemorations/royals/richard-ii-and-anne-of-bohemia

Magna Carta. David Carpenter. Penguin Classics. 2015.

The Welsh Wars of Edward I. John E. Morris. Da Capo. 1996. 1st ed 1901.

John of Gaunt. Sydney Armitage-Smith. Forgotten Books. 2020. 1st ed 1905.

Bomber Boys. Kevin Wilson. Orion. 2006.

The Divided Self. R.D. Laing. Penguin Modern Classics. 2010

Life and Fate. Vasily Grossman. Vintage Classics. 2006

Le Beat Bespoké vol 3, audio cd, 2008.

Aspect Design. 89 Newtown road, Malvern.

This book is dedicated to the
autodidactiiae

Bringing history to life!

To see all of our range visit
www.heritageplayingcards.com

Bringing history to life!